"You've Been Underestimating Me, Carla,"

Clay said quietly, "and if you do it again, you'll pay for it."

Carla swallowed hard, sensing that they were about to face-off in a brand-new, much more dangerous arena. He'd called her by her first name, establishing an intimacy that she wasn't sure she could handle. "I'll take that warning under advisement...Clay."

"You do that," he suggested, gratified by the trepidation in her eyes. She wasn't viewing him as a stodgy banker any longer but a force to be reckoned with, and he planned to make sure that perception didn't change.

Slowly, deliberately, he focused his eyes on her soft mouth. "Though I doubt the impetuous side of your nature will heed any kind of warning, it will be interesting to see which facet of your personality wins out in the end—the lady or the vamp."

Dear Reader:

Series and Spin-offs! Connecting characters and intriguing interconnections to make your head whirl.

In Joan Hohl's successful trilogy for Silhouette Desire—*Texas Gold* (7/86), *California Copper* (10/86), *Nevada Silver* (1/87)—Joan created a cast of characters that just wouldn't quit. You figure out how *Lady Ice* (5/87) connects. And in August, "J.B." demanded his own story—*One Tough Hombre*. In *Falcon's Flight*, coming in November, you'll learn *all* about...?

Annette Broadrick's *Return to Yesterday* (6/87) introduced Adam St. Clair. This August *Adam's Story* tells about the woman who saves his life—and teaches him a thing or two about love!

The six Branigan brothers appeared in Leslie Davis Guccione's *Bittersweet Harvest* (10/86) and *Still Waters* (5/87). September brings *Something in Common*, where the eldest of the strapping Irishmen finds love in unexpected places.

Midnight Rambler by Linda Barlow is in October—a special Halloween surprise, and totally unconnected to anything.

Keep an eye out for other Silhouette Desire favorites—Diana Palmer, Dixie Browning, Ann Major and Elizabeth Lowell, to name a few. You never know when secondary characters will insist on their own story....

All the best,

Isabel Swift
Senior Editor & Editorial Coordinator
Silhouette Books

JOYCE THIES
The Primrose Path

Silhouette Desire

Published by Silhouette Books New York

America's Publisher of Contemporary Romance

SILHOUETTE BOOKS
300 East 42nd St., New York, N.Y. 10017

Copyright © 1987 by Joyce Thies

ISBN: 0-373-05378-9

First Silhouette Books printing September 1987

America's Publisher of Contemporary Romance

Printed in the U.S.A.

Books by Joyce Thies

Silhouette Desire

* *Territorial Rights* #147
  Spellbound #348
  False Pretenses #359
  The Primrose Path #378

* written as Melissa Scott

JOYCE THIES

has been reading and writing romances since her teens but had to wait ten years before one was published. Since then she has authored or coauthored over twenty contemporary and historical novels. Readers might recognize her as the Joyce half of Janet Joyce. She wrote her first Silhouette Desire, *Territorial Rights*, as Melissa Scott, but is now writing under her own name.

She met her husband in college, and it was love at first sight. Joyce believes that out of sharing comes growth for both partners. She says, "Because of the loving man in my life, I've become everything I've ever wanted to be: wife, mother and writer. With each book I write, I imagine another woman lucky enough to have it all."

One

In the glory days of his adventurous youth, Frederick Valentine had earned the nickname "Freddie the Fleecer" because of his extraordinary talent for relieving unsuspecting marks of their money. He was now well past seventy and no longer allowed to practice his chosen profession, but he could still take pride in the knowledge that he hadn't lost the Midas touch. The average female cashier was just as susceptible to his old-world charm today as she'd been over forty years ago.

If not for his granddaughter's untimely interference, the prim, beetle-nosed woman with thinning hair who manned the cash register at the Palisades Diner would never have suspected him of being responsible for the shortage she'd find at the close of the day's business. A few gentlemanly remarks about her beau-

tiful eyes and attractive hairdo had eradicated all
thoughts of a swindle in progress. That was why
Freddie found it so galling to watch Carla pay the
woman every cent he'd just managed to shortchange
her.

He adored his granddaughter, but her disapproval
of any form of larceny was keeping him from having
any fun at all in his old age. He'd thought he'd out-
foxed her by sending her off to the ladies' room while
he'd paid the check for their lunch, but Carla had seen
right through that ploy. If he weren't so frustrated by
her diligent efforts to keep him on the straight and
narrow, he might have taken pride in her instincts. As
it was, all he could do was scowl at her as she exited
the restaurant and joined him for the short walk to his
apartment at Ridgeport, the exclusive retirement
complex overlooking the waters of the Great South
Bay.

"I'm the one who should be angry," Carla declared as she fell into step beside her grandfather.
Mindful of his tendency to punctuate his speech with
the blunt end of his hand carved walnut cane, she
stayed well out of range. "You promised me that
you'd be good."

"I'm not only good, I'm the best," Freddie retorted smugly, reaching up to tap the crown of his fe-
dora as he noted the amused grin Carla couldn't quite
hide. With a renewed spring in his step, he hooked the
curved end of his cane over his bent arm and quick-
ened his pace. There was hope for her yet.

If he played his cards right, one of these days Carla
would realize her full potential and accept the legacy

he wished to pass down to her. Stuffy Franklin and Dim Delores had done their level best to stifle their daughter's development as a free spirit, but that spirit was still there, just waiting to be set free. Freddie could see it in her eyes.

Sometimes when Carla thought he wasn't looking, those tranquil blue eyes of hers would sparkle with laughter and mischief. Hidden behind those serene, ladylike features was a woman with a rebellious nature and a mind like a steel trap. Even better, beneath those man-tailored business suits she always wore was the slim, curvaceous body of a born seductress.

Yesiree! Charlotte Katherine Valentine didn't know it yet, but she had the capacity to follow in his glorious footsteps. And oh, what a delightful path he intended to set for her.

"What am I going to do with you, Grandpa?" Carla sighed and shook her head, though the movement didn't loosen one strand of her silky brown hair from its tightly wound cornet.

"What harm did it do to charge that pitifully unattractive lady a small fee for the pleasure I gave her?" Freddie asked, employing the faulty logic that had eventually landed him in a prison cell for a term of two years. "For a couple of minutes there, that poor soul felt like a million bucks."

Resigned to the fact that she couldn't change her grandfather's thinking at this late date, Carla attacked on another front. Slipping one beautifully manicured hand into the deep pocket of her beige linen jacket, she pulled out a pair of loaded dice. She tossed them up in the air, then easily recaptured them in her palm. "In case you're thinking of arranging another big game tonight with your unsuspecting neighbors, keep in mind that I've confiscated these. I met George Byers in the hallway on my way to your apartment, and he told me he lost over twenty dollars to you last night. Since we both know how you came by your good fortune, I felt an obligation to return his money."

"That pompous old windbag was lucky I let him off so easily," Freddie muttered unrepentantly. "He thinks he's superior to everyone else just because his family came over on the Mayflower. Lords it over all of us every chance he gets. It did my heart good to take him down a peg using a game that was being played by our ancient Egyptian ancestors long before his lofty English relatives were even born."

Carla couldn't help but laugh. "Grandpa, just because your father claimed some Arabian blood and happened to be born in Cairo doesn't mean our family can be traced back to ancient Egypt."

"Doesn't mean it can't either," Freddie replied reasonably, brown eyes snapping with enthusiasm as he launched into one of his favorite topics of discussion. "I know for a fact that archaeologists have found crooked dice in the Egyptian burial grounds. The roots of my profession were established in the Golden Age over three thousand years ago. Aeons before those pious Puritans set sail, our illustrious relatives were winning and losing empires on the toss of the dice."

"Mother and Dad are going to be *so* happy to hear this," Carla remarked. "Instead of bragging that our family was there for the landing at Plymouth Rock, they can start telling people that our roots can be traced all the way back to ancient Egyptian hoods."

"Yes indeed." Freddie brandished the handle of his cane at her. "Haven't you ever wondered why your eyes are shaped the way they are?"

"My eyes!" Carla questioned. "What does the shape of my eyes have to do with anything?"

"Believe it or not, my girl," Freddie began, silver mustache twitching. "But Queen Nefertiti's eyes had the same exotic slant and almond shape as yours. Yes indeed, a blind man could see you've got her eyes."

"Funny, I thought my eyes were passed on to me from mother's side of the family."

Freddie dismissed that claim with another nonchalant flourish of his cane. "I suppose Delores can take credit for passing on that blue color, but I'd be willing to bet everything I own that the shape came down from the ancient queen herself."

Since Carla was her grandfather's sole source of financial support, she knew that would be a safe bet, but she cared too much about him and his pride to mention that. Besides, even thinking about the farfetched possibility of being related to a historically renowned beauty such as Nefertiti gave her a tiny thrill of pleasure. It wasn't often that a rather plain, straitlaced and conservative C.P.A. got to think of herself as a descendant of ancient royalty.

The opportunity for experiencing these unexpected enjoyments was one of the main reasons she hadn't closed the door in Freddie's face when this fascinating, silver-haired and silver-tongued skeleton had walked out of the family closet and into her life. Up until that fateful day, Carla had assumed that both of her paternal grandparents had died long before her birth. According to the story told by her equally plain, straitlaced and conservative parents, Frederick Valentine was a no-account rounder who in the late 1930s had deserted his pregnant wife, Katherine Tate-Valentine, in order to pursue a life of petty crime. Not long afterward, Katherine had died giving birth to a son.

The elder Tates had immediately determined that Katherine's child would be better off never knowing his wastrel of a father. Since Franklin was the only male child produced by the Boston branch of the family, the Tates had gladly assumed full responsibility for his upbringing. Frederick Valentine had been declared dead and the old-moneyed family had never mentioned his name again. Unfortunately, no one had informed Frederick of his demise and two years ago, he'd had the bad manners to prove himself very much alive.

Carla had been so shocked when he'd announced his identity, that she'd opened the door of her apartment to him, and within minutes, she'd also opened the door of her heart. Much to the dismay of her parents, she'd not only listened to her grandfather's side of the story, she'd believed it.

Frederick Valentine had never loved Katherine Tate though she'd pursued him with a single-minded vengeance. He'd succumbed to her seductive charms only once, making it quite clear to her beforehand that making love wasn't a prelude to making promises.

Even so, when she'd told him of her pregnancy, he'd felt honor bound to marry her.

Less than three months after the ceremony, Katherine Tate had decided that marriage to a charming ne'er-do-well was as unacceptable to her as it was to her parents. Admitting that she'd lied about her condition, she'd told Freddie to leave so she could return to the comfortable bosom of her wealthy family. Unfortunately, neither she nor Frederick had known that subsequent to their short-term marriage, Katherine's lie about being pregnant had become a reality.

For the next three years, Freddie had lived in New York, expecting but never receiving Katherine's declaration of divorce. Eventually, he'd contacted Jason Bellamy, senior partner in the firm of lawyers retained to handle all legal matters for the Tates. Bellamy had coldly informed him that Katherine had died giving birth to a son and that Freddie, by virtue of his desertion, had given up all claim to the child. The lawyer had convinced Freddie that he could never win in a custody battle with the powerful Tates. Any judge would decree that young master Valentine was much better off in the care of his wealthy, upstanding grandparents than in that of his shiftless father.

Considering what a boring man her father had turned out to be, Carla would not have agreed with the judge. Under the supposedly beneficial auspices of his grandparents, Franklin had been taught to be a snob—a cold, haughty man who never strayed from convention in thought, word or deed. Like almost all other Tates before him, Franklin followed the dictates of his elders without question. His grandparents had determined what schools he would attend, what position he would occupy in the family shipping firm and what woman he would marry. Even after their deaths, Franklin had never once attempted to stray from the pattern they'd outlined for him at birth.

On the other hand, his father, Frederick Xavier Valentine, thumbed his nose at convention and formed new patterns for himself every day. He was unlike any person Carla had ever known. In a mundane world of dull routine and social dictates, Freddie was a weaver of whimsical dreams, a free-spirited gypsy who followed no one's rules but his own. To him, each day marked the start of a new adventure in which he could do anything and be anyone he chose.

Depending on his audience, Freddie could assume the dulcet tones of a literary scholar, the lilting brogue of an Irish leprechaun or the cultured accent of an English lord. A consummate actor, he lived by his wits, and until he'd been forced into retirement by an unsympathetic judge, he'd prospered by the knowledge that a little bit of trickery existed in everyone.

Try as she might, Carla couldn't quite convince him to stop taking advantage of that knowledge. She lived in fear that one day he would do something she wasn't able to fix and be sent back to prison. Unable to bear the thought of that happening, she'd done all she could to provide him with everything he might need to be content. Financially, she supposed she was as much a victim of his renowned charm as any of his previous marks, but she hadn't regretted one cent of the money she'd spent on him thus far.

Her grandfather had given her a new outlook on life and taught her to stop taking herself so seriously. He'd shown her that if she just loosened up a bit and ventured out of her shell, the world could be her oyster too. Slowly, she was coming to understand that even a mature, responsible woman of twenty-seven, owner of a highly successful accounting firm, deserved to kick up her heels occasionally. For a person whose childhood memories didn't include having fun without a more constructive purpose being served at the same time, doing something for the sheer joy of it was an alien concept.

At the moment, however, Carla didn't have time to dwell on what fun things she might do when she finally gave herself that well-deserved vacation. It was nearing the fifteenth of April, the busiest time of the year for an accountant. If her grandfather hadn't called to say he had an important announcement to make, a stick of dynamite couldn't have removed her from her Manhattan office. In the past two years, however, she'd learned that Freddie's announcements usually wreaked more havoc in her life than a stick of dynamite ever could, and she'd made the long drive out to the south shore of Long Island in record time.

"So?" she inquired, bracing herself for the worst. "How much longer do you intend to keep me in suspense?"

"Timing is everything, my dear," Freddie returned smoothly. "You were much too uptight over lunch to grasp the full import of what I'm about to tell you. You really must learn to relax and enjoy yourself."

Carla drew in a calming breath. "Sorry, but this is as relaxed as I'm going to get until tax time is over."

Giving the government its due had never come high on Freddie's list of priorities, but he understood why Carla gave the matter so much of her attention. She made a very good living at it, a much better living than he'd ever achieved attempting to hoodwink Uncle Sam. Unfortunately, Carla had dedicated herself to her profession to the exclusion of all else. It was his duty to show her that there were many other, far more pleasurable things she could do in this life.

Freddie tapped his cane on the sidewalk, making sure he had her full attention. "I promise not to keep you any longer than it takes to request your presence at a dinner party being given this evening at the ancestral home of my intended."

"Your intended what?"

Freddie's brows rose. "My intended wife, of course."

As bombshells went, this was one of his better ones Carla thought with grudging admiration as she searched for the closest place to sit down. She was grateful to find herself within groping distance of one of the white wrought-iron benches that graced the sweeping, landscaped lawns of the retirement complex. Once safely seated, she managed weakly, "You did say wife?"

"Indeed I did," Freddie admitted gleefully as he sat down beside her. "And I felt sure you'd want to be present tonight at the family gathering when we make our engagement official."

Carla knew better than to voice her true feelings over this announcement until her grandfather had revealed the full extent of his latest plan to drive her insane. "This is all rather sudden isn't it?"

Freddie made a theatrical gesture with his hand. "One never knows when or where Cupid's arrow shall strike. For me, it occurred two weeks ago right here on these grounds. Lilly is the new resident in 4-A. As luck would have it, she was assigned to be my partner for a game of shuffleboard. It turned out to be a match made in heaven."

"Lilly?"

"My angelic ladylove, Lillian Northrop Chancelor," Freddie answered, supplying the full name of his fiancée. Then he leaned back and waited for the result.

It came immediately. Carla closed her eyes and groaned, "Please tell me we're not talking Chancelor as in banks."

With a triumphant sparkle in his lively brown eyes, Freddie confirmed, "As in banks. As in international investments and commercial properties. As in a magnificent family estate nestled between mansions out in the Hamptons."

After a long eloquent silence, Carla breathed, "You know I can't let you do this, Grandpa."

"Why ever not? The woman absolutely adores me."

"And you absolutely adore her money."

"Nonsense," Freddie insisted fervently, patting her hand. "If Lillian were utterly penniless, I would still wish to spend all the remaining days of my life with her."

Carla never ceased to be amazed at her grandfather's knack for telling whoppers like this one with a totally straight face. "If you don't give up this ridiculous notion, you just might spend all the remaining days of your life in the less than charming company of the state of New York prison system."

Freddie had the audacity to look offended. "As far as I know, falling in love has never been considered a crime."

"I doubt that the Chancelors will see it that way if you try and take advantage of a member of their family."

"I would never take advantage of such a fine lady as Lillian. When you meet her, you'll understand that we were destined to be together."

Carla responded with one of the more expressive words from Freddie's oftentimes archaic vocabulary. "Balderdash!"

"I'm surprised at you, Carla. As a single woman, you know very well what it's like to be lonely."

"You've never had a lonely day in your life."

Freddie put on a sad face, knowing that she would never believe him if he disputed her statement. And it wouldn't help his present cause any if Carla knew that he'd been very lonely until he'd met a repressed young woman with beautiful blue eyes and his blood running through her veins. She had opened her heart to a broken-down old man, loved him unconditionally and given him a new lease on life.

For that, she deserved the best and Freddie was going to make sure she got it. "I would think you'd be happy that I'd found someone with whom I can share my declining years."

"Pure poppycock," Carla declared unsympathetically.

Freddie threw up his hands. "I was hoping to have your blessing, but..." His voice trailed off meaningfully.

Sensing that he was firmly committed to this outrageous plan, Carla lost control. "I'm warning you, Grandpa. You won't get away with this! The Chancelors are about as blue-blooded as they come. As soon as they find out about your nefarious past, happy days are over."

Freddie shrugged off that risk with a complacent grin. "But meanwhile, won't we have some grand fun?"

"Not if I have anything to say about it!"

"My dear, at times you can be such a stick-in-the-mud that I can hardly believe we're related."

"And you can be such an unprincipled rascal, at times I wish we weren't," Carla retorted.

"Should I take that to mean you can't make it to this evening's affair?" Freddie asked.

"On the contrary," Carla protested, "I wouldn't miss it for the world."

Barclay Northrop Chancelor III arrived home late for dinner. Normally, that would not have caused either him or any member of his family a moment's concern. Tonight, however, as he entered the formal dining room, Barclay Northrop Chancelor II scraped back his chair and greeted his thirty-three year old son with the kind of question Clay hadn't heard since he'd been a teenager.

"Dammit Clay! Where the devil have you been?"

Before he could reply to that startling inquiry, Clay was hit with a direct order from his mother, Georgine, who appeared to be on the verge of tears. "I insist you do something about this, Barclay—and I do mean immediately!"

"Of course, Mother." Noting the presence of strangers at the table, Clay felt a flush of embarrassment creep up his neck. Though he still didn't have a clue as to what was going on here, he highly resented being called on the carpet like a tardy schoolboy.

For a brief moment, his gaze slid to the somberly dressed young woman seated to the left of his mother and his color deepened. She wore the tight bun and disapproving expression of an old-fashioned schoolmarm. On the other hand, the expression worn by the nattily dressed, elderly man seated to her right was one of unbridled amusement. Clay wasn't thrilled by either reaction.

Who the hell were these people, anyway? They didn't look like the type his parents would go out of their way to impress. After putting in an exhausting twelve-hour day at the bank, Clay didn't feel like making small talk with two people he didn't know and would probably never see again, but it was becoming increasingly obvious that he was expected to do just that.

Looking neither to the right nor left as he strode across the room, Clay didn't notice that there was a fourth person present at the table. Jaws clenched, he took his customary seat, which placed him across from their two guests. After hastily rebuttoning the top button of his starched white shirt, he straightened his silk tie, then said politely, "I apologize to everyone for being late. I was unaware that we were having company this evening."

"Northrop?" Georgine cast a withering look at her husband.

"I'm sure I told him at breakfast," Northrop growled, still glaring at his son who was beginning to feel as if he'd just stepped into some kind of time warp and had been regressed to the age of ten.

"We haven't spoken today," Clay reminded his father, his irritation growing.

"Nevertheless, it wouldn't hurt you to show up here on time once in a while," Northrop stated, seemingly oblivious to the fact that he was behaving entirely out of character by actually raising his cultured voice in the presence of strangers. "After all, we are your only family and in the event of a crisis, it would be nice to know we could rely on your presence. I must say—"

"Your apology is accepted, dear," a saner voice interrupted Northrop's speech.

Clay had never been more grateful to hear that gently modulated tone. He had no idea why his parents were behaving so strangely, but felt sure that his grandmother was about to cast some light on the situation. His welcoming smile shone down the length of the polished mahogany table to where she was seated.

"Clay, I would like you to meet Frederick Valentine and his granddaughter, Charlotte," Lillian Northrop Chancelor, the always gracious, always elegant matriarch of the family stated calmly as if nothing was amiss.

Before Clay could acknowledge the introduction, his mother rendered him speechless by covering her face in her hands and crying, "It's shocking, Clay! What they're planning is just too shocking for words! You've got to do something!"

Beginning to get desperate, Clay turned to his grandmother, his hazel eyes silently pleading for help. Lillian accepted his look with a radiant smile. "It's all really very simple, dear. You see, Frederick and I have just announced our engagement."

It took several seconds for her words to sink in, but when they did, Clay understood why his normally reserved parents were so upset. Sometime today, while he'd been hard at work in his midtown office, his sweet little seventy-two-year-old grandmother had gone stark, raving mad.

Two

As Northrop Chancelor escorted his distraught wife out one set of double French doors, Frederick Valentine hurriedly ushered his tearful fiancée out the other. In the deadly silence that followed this mass exodus, Carla sat motionless in her chair, staring at the hand-painted design on her bone china place setting. The only other remaining occupant of the dining room was observing her just as intently as she studied the china, but with far less appreciation. Clay Chancelor was viewing her as if she were something that had just crawled out from beneath a rock.

He might consider her a lowlife, but a different term came to mind when Carla looked at him. Beautiful! Having grown up around his type, she'd expected him to be something of a snob, suave, sophisticated and urbane, but she hadn't expected him to be so absolutely beautiful.

He looked like a Michelangelo sculpture dressed in a navy, three-piece suit. Tall, slender, he had dark hazel eyes and glowing jet-black hair. His nose was aquiline, mouth perfect and his jaw could have been chiseled out of marble. The instant he'd entered the room, Carla had lost all power of speech.

Unaware that his eyes mirrored his feelings, nor that his anger with himself was being aimed at the woman seated across from him, Clay cursed the day when he'd agreed to his grandmother's request to live with people her own age. Less than a month after moving in at Ridgeport, she'd gone and gotten herself engaged to a seemingly charming old duffer who'd probably started counting her money the instant he'd recognized her name.

After hearing his grandmother's announcement, Clay had subjected the man to a closer scrutiny and had quickly determined that Frederick Valentine might look very dapper but the material of his suit was a cheap polyester blend. The man's vacuous granddaughter was wearing a shapeless sack of a dress bought straight off the rack. Knowing what kind of rent was being charged at Ridgeport, Clay concluded that Valentine was one of the few charity cases accepted at the exclusive complex.

Evidently, Frederick had met Lillian and quickly realized that he needn't keep his living requirements within the limits of his meager pension. To enjoy the good life, all he had to do was marry the bank.

Somehow Clay had to keep that from happening—but how? Lillian Chancelor had always had a mind of her own. If she intended to marry again, that's exactly what she would do. Look at what had happened when she'd decided that her son wasn't handling the family business in the way she felt it should be handled? Within a week she'd signed over her voting power to Clay, which had placed him in sole charge of Chancelor Enterprises. Clay knew that in order to stop her from signing everything else over to a total stranger, he was going to have to proceed very cautiously.

When she could bear the awful silence no longer, Carla spoke. "Nice weather we're having, isn't it?" Her weak attempt at humor failed miserably. Showing no sign that he'd even heard her, the man kept right on staring as if she were some slithery, slimy form of earthworm.

Considering the semihysterical scene that had just taken place, Carla could understand his being upset, but that didn't give him the right to judge an innocent spectator so harshly. It wasn't her fault that his mother had practically prostrated herself on the dinner table or that his father had made an absolute fool out of himself with his blustering. She wasn't responsible for this mess. Oh no, the real guilty party had excused both himself and his elderly ladylove at the earliest available opportunity.

In the very near future, Carla planned to have a few pithy words with Freddie on that subject, but in the meantime she was going to use the same tone on someone else. No matter how far above her this man assumed himself to be, she was growing extremely tired of being studied like larvae under a high-powered microscope. "Listen! Instead of sitting here glaring daggers at me, why don't we try something more constructive like figuring out what we're going to do about this ridiculous situation."

Having long since forgotten her presence, Clay blinked at the sound of the woman's voice. It took him another second or two to digest her words. "We? What *we* are going to do?"

Carla expelled an exasperated breath and gestured to the empty room. "Do you see anyone else around? If we don't do something, who will?"

It was as if a light had suddenly switched on in his head. The anger faded from his eyes and was replaced by wary speculation. "Okay, I think I see where you're coming from."

"I was sure that you would." Carla nodded approvingly.

"Might I ask why you're approaching me and not some other member of the family?" Clay asked.

"Because you're the man in charge."

That startled him. "What makes you think that?"

Carla scoffed at his tone of surprise. "It's common knowledge in financial circles—your father is still chairman, but you control the family holdings. Your grandmother signed over voting power of her block of shares three years ago during that crisis you had with your foreign investment company. I have to assume that she passed the corporate reins over to you because she has a lot of faith in your judgment. From there it was natural to conclude that the two of you must be very close."

"Very close." Clay reinforced her conclusion in a tone that sounded remarkably like a threat.

Carla immediately offered reassurance. "Please don't worry. You have my word that I'm as anxious as you are to resolve this problem without hurting your grandmother."

"I'm very grateful to hear that," Clay managed without sounding too sarcastic.

Carla appreciated his familial concern and smiled at him for the first time. She was completely unaware of the impact of that smile.

As Carla's lips tilted upwards, Clay saw what he'd been too preoccupied to notice before. He suddenly became aware of the tempting shape of her mouth, the exotic slant to her eyes, the fiery highlights in her tightly bound hair. His eyes slid lower.

A perfect oval face that was practically devoid of makeup revealed a flawless complexion. She wore a high collar, but it couldn't quite hide her slender neck. Several more inches down, he made the most damning discovery yet. Her shapeless gray dress did a commendable job but couldn't quite camouflage a magnificent figure!

Now that he was looking at her, really looking, he realized that he wasn't dealing with some poor mousy creature who was counting her blessings over this sudden turn of good fortune, but a professional she-wolf out for blood. To keep the wool pulled over everyone's eyes long enough for her geriatric accomplice to complete his portion of their business, she had deliberately downplayed her most provocative features.

In his younger days, Clay had dealt with several beautiful but avaricious women who'd tried to establish contact with his bank account by attempting to steal his heart. Since then, he hadn't had much time to waste on women and romance, but he imagined there were many who still considered him to be one of the country's most eligible bachelors.

Unlike the seductive gold diggers he'd dealt with in the past, this clever little number and her partner had taken them unawares by sneaking into the family vault through the back door. Who would ever have thought that his elderly grandmother would be considered as good a catch as he was? Only a very shrewd operator, that's who. This woman had played them all for fools, and he was about to learn how much it was going to cost him.

To Carla's amazement, just when she thought they were starting to make some progress, the man's gaze had turned insolent again. Actually, the way he was looking at her was more than insolent, it was downright insulting. With one burning glance, he stripped off her clothes and swiftly passed judgment on her female attributes. When his gaze drifted slowly up to her face, they gleamed with an unmistakable message. She had nothing he wanted.

Carla didn't care to know why he'd suddenly taken such an interest in her figure. Nor did she care to let him know how much his conclusion hurt. She realized that she wasn't the most attractive woman in the world, but no man had ever looked at her as if she had absolutely nothing to offer.

Cheeks burning, she chose to ignore his humiliating message and return his attention to where it belonged. "I don't quite know where you stand on this, but I hope you'll join me in doing whatever's necessary to prevent this marriage from taking place."

"And we both know what's necessary, don't we?" Clay bit out sarcastically as he pushed back his chair and stood up. "By all means, let's talk terms. Then you'll know exactly where I stand."

"Terms?" Carla asked, confused. "What do you mean by terms?"

"You can quit the act, lady! I've got the picture!" Clay snapped as he rounded the table.

"Quit what act?" Carla wanted to know, but could see by his face that her question had only made him more angry. She didn't know what had set him off again, but as she watched his long-legged approach she began to get frightened. The man simply exuded power. It was there in his glittering dark eyes, in the stubborn set of his jaw and the grim outline of the most masculine-looking mouth she'd ever seen.

She gasped in shock when his fingers closed like a vise around her arm. "Now wait just a minute here!" she cried out, but that didn't stop him from pulling her rudely up out of her chair.

"Come on," Clay ordered, hauling her unceremoniously behind him.

"Come on where?" Carla demanded, for all the good it did her. In a matter of seconds, she was hustled out of the room, down a long hallway, and into another room that appeared to be a private study. As soon as they were inside, Clay dropped her arm, then turned his back on her in order to lock the door.

Carla used the short respite to massage away the pain and to study her new surroundings. Unlike the feminine Louis XIV furnishings of the dining room, this room was done in masculine brown leathers and dark, gleaming woods. Floor-to-ceiling bookshelves, each containing what looked to be a priceless collection of leather-bound editions, lined three of the walls. The fourth was paneled in rich mahogany and it housed a low, glass-enclosed fireplace. A huge, ornately framed oil painting hung over the mantel.

Since the man in the picture so closely resembled the man who had just dragged her protesting body into this room, Carla assumed the portrait was of Barclay the First, Lillian Chancelor's late husband, renowned land speculator, respected investment broker and the founding father of the Chancelor Bank. She had to admit that the dark-haired, dark-eyed autocrat peering down at her was an impressive looking ancestor. Almost as impressive looking as the third-generation despot who had taken up his position behind a large desk and was now issuing an imperious order for her to be seated in one of the two leather chairs facing him.

Carla followed his dictate, not because she felt intimidated, but because she couldn't wait to hear what he had to say next. In the few moments that had passed since he'd mentioned "talking terms," she'd figured out what he must be thinking. The presumptuous man assumed she was about to make an attempt to extort money from him. If only her grandfather wasn't her grandfather, she would have found that assumption laughable.

A few seconds later, Carla was beyond laughter. Clay Chancelor opened the middle drawer of the desk and pulled out a checkbook. "Okay, honey," he began in the most insulting tone any man had ever used on her. "If you'd offered me that luscious body of yours, I might have taken you up on it. I might even have come up with an expensive trinket or two in payment for your delightful services, but you knew that would be the bottom line, didn't you? Therefore, within limits, I'm prepared to reward you for having the intelligence to go after my grandmother instead of me. Name your price."

Carla couldn't decide how to react to his astounding speech. It was one thing for him to think that she was part of some extortion plot, but quite another to hear herself described in such degrading terms. In his position, he probably saw blackmail schemes developing around every corner. Knowing the sizable amount of his family's fortune, Carla could almost forgive him for jumping to that kind of conclusion.

However, for him to think that she, an ultraconservative, certified public accountant, with a background highly similar to his own, was capable of selling her body was incredible. Beyond that, the knowledge that if she'd made the offer, he might very well have accepted, completely boggled her mind. Luscious! Men rarely noticed that she even had a body, but this man had not only noticed, he thought it luscious.

"Come on, beautiful," Clay urged. "You're a pro and we both know you've backed me into a corner, so tell me what kind of number you had in mind."

Carla shook her head in bemusement as a long-suppressed imp inside her surged to life. This was getting better every minute. "Not only luscious but beautiful," she mused, blue eyes shining with inner mirth. "I really should give you a discount just for the compliments."

Clay gritted his teeth as she dropped the schoolmarm guise and revealed her true nature. Even though he'd been expecting it, he was still shocked by the transformation. Suddenly, her placid blue eyes were shimmering like precious sapphires and a delicate shade of pink touched her colorless cheeks. She smiled at him like the temptress she was, tantalizing him with a glimpse of thigh as she crossed her shapely legs.

He forced his eyes back to her face and met her amused gaze. Incensed by her knowing smirk, he bit off the words. "Quit stalling, honey. I want you out of here."

When she spoke again even her voice had changed. Each word was like the stroke of soft, warm velvet against oversensitized skin. "Even a very wealthy man doesn't always get what he wants. Or hasn't anyone ever taught you that valuable lesson?"

Clay felt the racing of his heart that preceded arousal. Though completely out of his realm of experience, this woman was beautiful. Passion and adventure shimmered in her gaze, enticing him. Gazing into those exotic eyes, Clay realized that she'd probably enjoyed the kind of sexual encounters that he'd only imagined in his most erotic fantasies.

Unable to help himself, his eyes wandered over her face, down to the moist pink outline of her full mouth. "Are you offering to teach me something I don't know, Ms. Valentine?"

Carla didn't think she'd ever enjoyed herself more in her life. "It would be my pleasure, Mr. Chancelor," she drawled softly. "And just to show you how generous I am, tonight's lesson will be free of charge."

Clay wondered how many other wealthy men she'd victimized like this and how many had gotten to enjoy her gorgeous body before they'd found out the score. If he made love to her, at least he'd know what he was getting.

He was amazed at himself for even considering such an idea, but something inside him refused to back down from her dare. She might consider him a stuffy, unimaginative banker, but he still knew how to pleasure a woman. Perhaps he could teach her a few things, as well.

He reached for a pen to write down her address. "When and where, sweetheart?"

"Here and now, darling."

Clay dropped the pen. "What! We can't just—"

"I can, and you won't even have to get up from your desk," Carla challenged, then leaned back in her chair as all the blood drained out of his face. Clay Chancelor had done more to inflate her ego in the past few minutes than any other man had ever done. Who would've thought she could pull off an act like this? Especially with a sophisticated man like this?

Basking in her newfound feminine power, she couldn't resist going one step further. She batted her eyelashes and purred, "It should only take a couple of minutes."

Clay gulped at her confident statement and his face turned beet-red. Her estimation of his staying power was almost as deflating as her outrageous proposition. For the first time in his life, he was dealing with a woman who was so far out of his depth he didn't have a clue how to handle her. Her sparkling eyes dared him to either sink or swim and he knew it was sink.

Carla watched Clay squirm for a moment, then burst out laughing. Her grandfather had predicted they would have some grand fun before the blue-blooded Chancelors squashed his plan, but fool that she was, she hadn't believed him.

"I don't see what's so damned funny, you little—"

"I'm sorry." Carla brought her laughter under control, sensing that she'd amused herself at this man's expense long enough.

"Sure you are," he ground out, still seething.

"Believe me, Mr. Chancelor, I'm not out after your money or your body," she stated. "I'm afraid you've misjudged both me and this situation. Actually, all I wanted was for you to help me think of some way to keep our grandparents from getting married. Since I couldn't come up with any good ideas myself, I was hoping you could. You see, I don't like the prospect of their marriage any better than you do."

Still chafing from her mocking laughter, Clay raged, "You really expect me to believe that stupid story?"

"It's the truth," she replied simply, then making note of his mottled complexion, accepted the possibility that she'd taken her teasing a tad too far. If she'd had more experience dealing with men, she might have been more knowledgeable about the care and handling of the male ego. Clay Chancelor looked like he was searching for any excuse to do murder.

"I apologize for embarrassing you," she repeated hastily, frightened by the intensity of his glare. "I was only pulling your leg."

"You were doing more than pulling my leg and you damned well know it!"

Carla blushed at his words and shot back defensively, "It's not my fault that you're so oversexed."

"Oversexed! Come off it, honey! You're the one who proposed I just sit back and enjoy it."

"Exactly my point," Carla retorted, offended by his censorious tone. "I came here to make a perfectly innocent request and look how you reacted. You force me into a locked room and make one indecent suggestion after another. Is this how you treat all your female guests?"

Barclay Northrop Chancelor III, who was far too civilized to resort to violence, pounded his fist on the surface of the desk and shouted, "What kind of game are you playing now, lady? Just how big of an idiot do you think I am?"

Charlotte Katherine Valentine, who was much too refined to raise her voice, shouted back, "Considering who you think I am, I would say you're a huge one!"

Clay shot up out of his chair. "And you're nothing but a cheap tramp out to earn a fast buck!"

Carla shot up out of hers. "Well you're a conceited, arrogant snob whose brain is smaller than his wallet!"

Their angry voices filtered through the locked door to the elderly couple who stood listening on the other side.

"Get out!" Clay bellowed.

"Gladly!" Carla shrieked.

Freddie grinned with Lillian at the sound of sensible pumps marching toward the door.

"And if you know what's good for you, you won't come back!"

Lillian smiled at Freddie as they watched the doorknob turn with no result.

"For me to come back here, you'd have to get down on your hands and knees and beg!"

Freddie placed his arm over his fiancée's shoulders and guided her swiftly through the nearest set of double doors. "Sounds highly promising to me."

"Yes, indeed," Lillian agreed as they stepped into the drawing room.

Three

By the first of May, Carla had compiled, computed and signed all the required government forms for every one of her clients who was filing late tax returns. She'd broken all previous records completing this annual ritual and she had Barclay Northrop Chancelor III to thank for it. After her abortive meeting with that arrogant jerk, she'd given Freddie the Fleecer her blessing to fleece away, then thrown herself into her work.

For the next three weeks, she'd lived off the energy of an all-consuming anger, refusing to admit that she was more upset with herself than she was with Clay Chancelor or her scoundrel of a grandfather. But whoever was most responsible, the result of her single-minded attention to her work was being caught up on every one of her accounts. So caught up in fact that she could easily stay out of the office for a full month without falling behind again.

Late Friday afternoon, as Carla sat behind her desk contemplating that daunting prospect, her secretary buzzed through on the intercom. "What is it, Leslie?"

"Carla, there's a man out here who insists on seeing you. He doesn't have an appointment, but . . . hey!"

Carla's spine went rigid at Leslie's exclamation and stiffened further as the door to her office burst open. Recognizing her visitor, she resisted the urge to lift her fingers to her hair and assure herself that no tendrils had worked loose from the precisely positioned coil at her nape. Nor, as much as she would have liked the additional armor, did she attempt to cover her white pleated silk blouse with the black plaid jacket hanging over the back of her chair. She simply leaned over the intercom and stated stiffly, "It's all right, Leslie. I've been expecting Mr. Chancelor."

Upon receiving her secretary's relieved response, Carla lifted her finger to cut off communication with the outer office. Judging by his expression as he walked through the door, round two of their battle was about to begin. Going by her last humiliating skirmish with this man, she didn't want another living soul listening in on it. She dearly hoped that she would make a better showing this time than she had the last.

"I'll just bet you've been expecting me," Clay announced sarcastically as he marched across the room and dropped a thick set of documents onto her desk. He then dropped himself into the closest chair. "Read it and weep."

Carla didn't have to read anything to know what had prompted his visit, and she'd never felt less like crying. The instant he'd stepped through the door, she'd felt a surge of adrenaline racing through her veins and a rush of some other hormone she didn't care to name. Clay Chancelor was just as beautiful as the last time she'd seen him and her reaction to his looks was still the same.

She liked what she saw far too much and, since it was obvious that he wasn't suffering a similar reaction to the sight of her, that placed her at a distinct disadvantage. Today he was dressed in a charcoal-gray suit and a crisp white shirt, both tailor-made. His tie was a deep maroon silk patterned with diagonal gray pinstripes, and there was a maroon silk pocket square peeking out of his expensive suit jacket. Except for the barbarous glow in his dark hazel eyes, he was a picture of polished European elegance.

Shoring up her inner defenses, Carla inquired, "So, how much did your investigation cost you?"

"Plenty and it was worth every penny," Clay retorted smugly. "Frederick Valentine is a con man!"

Just as smugly, Carla shot back, "I know, and I'm delighted to hear that you paid through the nose to find out."

On the drive to her office, Clay had promised himself that he would not let this woman get under his skin as he had the last time, but he could feel it happening again. She wasn't even slightly intimidated at being confronted with the damning evidence he'd gathered on her relation. Of course, his investigation hadn't presented him with a single fact he could use against her personally, but considering that her grandfather was an ex-con, she could at least show some discomfort.

She didn't. In fact, she looked very pleased with herself. As much as Clay hated to admit it, his anger and frustration with her was tempered by a certain amount of admiration. "You're a pretty cool customer, lady, but I'm on to you now and this sweet little scam you've got working won't land you anything but a nice long haul in the slammer!"

Satisfied that he'd laid out her options in language she couldn't misunderstand, Clay sat back to enjoy the result. He'd waited three long weeks for this moment, and he planned to savor it. No woman had ever made him feel as much a fool as this one had, but now he would have his revenge.

Carla cocked her head to one side, her expression curious. "Have you developed some weird kind of obsession with Al Capone since we last met?"

Clay was dumbfounded by the question.

"No?" Carla inquired at his perplexed silence. "Then why are you talking like some two-bit gangster?"

Clay muttered an explicit curse as the blood rushed into his face.

Carla flushed at his crudeness. "If you wish to continue this conversation, you can keep a civil tongue in your head!"

They glared at each other for several long seconds without speaking, but then Clay nodded. No matter how he felt about her, he was ashamed of himself for making such remarks to a woman. At the same time, her response to them made him smile. "I might sound like Al Capone, but you sound like Queen Victoria."

Lifting his nose in the air, he mimicked. "Keep a civil tongue in your head, Knave!"

Carla considered his accusation, then sighed in resignation. Sometimes, when she was under stress, she did sound a lot like her mother, who not only talked but acted like the late queen of England. "We do make quite a pair, don't we?"

"That's an understatement."

Not quite able to force back the smile tugging at her lips, Carla said, "I can see the headlines now, Mad monarch murders maniacal mobster."

Clay forgot that he despised this woman and burst out laughing. Carla failed to recall that she despised him back and joined in. By the time they regained control of themselves, neither of them found it easy to return to battle stations.

Annoyed with himself for being so easily captivated by her unexpected sense of humor, Clay was the first to make the attempt. He had come for one purpose and that purpose had nothing to do with his illogical attraction to this woman. After today, he hoped he'd be able to wipe her out of his mind. "I'm not here to make friends with you."

"I know why you're here," Carla replied. "And I don't like you, either."

Clay grinned. "Well, now that we've got that established, let's talk about how we're going to stop your grandfather from marrying my grandmother."

Carla's brows rose as she recalled having made the same request of him in the not so distant past. "We? How *we* are going to stop him?"

His grin growing wider, Clay gestured to the empty room. "Do you see anyone else around? If we don't, who will?"

Carla didn't respond to that engaging smile. It was obvious that his memory of their first encounter was just as vivid as her own, but unlike him, she wasn't willing to simply laugh it off. Clay Chancelor brought out the worst in her, and weeks later, she still couldn't understand what had possessed her to act the way she had.

This time, however, she vowed silently, she would stay in control no matter what kind of nasty accusations he threw her way. "After thinking it over, I don't see what either one of us can do. Our grandparents are both single and over twenty-one."

"Way over," Clay acknowledged heavily, then cleared his throat and launched into the carefully thought-out speech he'd prepared for this occasion, minus the gangster terminology he'd employed previously. "But their age isn't the main issue here, Ms. Valentine. Your grandfather is toying with my grandmother's affections for no other reason than financial gain and you damned well know it."

Pointing at the incriminating documents on her desk, he went on purposefully, "I'm sure you don't want me going public with the information contained in that report. You've got a thriving little business going here, and we both know what that kind of exposure would do to your list of clients. I'm also quite sure that your family would rather not have their dirty linen washed in public. Your mother could never show her face again in D.A.R. meetings. Therefore, you're going to do whatever I want you to do to end this farce."

Carla resented the fact that Clay knew all there was to know about her, but she had to admire the ruthlessness on his face and in his tone. She was certain that a large majority of people would have caved in immediately. Of course, knowing what her grandfather was like, she was obliged to lend Clay whatever assistance she could, but before they joined forces, she intended to prove she wasn't as stupid as he obviously thought.

"We're not going to accomplish anything if you persist in insulting my intelligence," she warned coldly. "While it's true that I'd rather not read about my grandfather's past exploits in the paper, we're both aware that I and my family are not the only ones who'd be hurt by it. How do you think your grandmother would react to the disclosure? Or for that matter, your parents? Somehow, I don't think they'd deal very well with the inevitable scandal, do you?"

Clay's lips tightened, disappointed but not surprised that she'd seen right through his empty threat. He met the scathing glint in her eye with a slightly sheepish grin. "You have to admit, it was worth a try."

Carla conceded the point. "If I were in your place, I would've done the same."

"And thereby, insulted *my* intelligence," Clay admonished.

"Yes," Carla conceded that point, too. "So, now that we've admitted that we're not likely to outwit each other, where do we go from here?"

"I guess that depends on whether you're part of the problem or a participant in the solution."

Carla frowned. "Meaning?"

Clay leaned back farther in his chair, unconsciously putting more distance between them as he said, "Maybe you and your grandfather are more than just kindred spirits. How do I know that you're not a silent partner in his plans? Beneath that conservative front you put on beats the heart of an adventuress. I've seen her in action and she's hardly the boring, sedate type I'd expect to be content with the tedious work required of an accountant."

Before Carla could voice the protest he saw poised on her lips, Clay held up his hand. "Oh, I'm well aware that your firm is legitimate, but you can't tell me your work satisfies all the requirements of your intrepid personality. So tell me, Ms. Valentine, when you lay down your calculator, what is it you do for excitement?"

Carla struggled to come up with an appropriate response. For some strange reason, this man refused to believe that she was exactly what she appeared to be both inside and out. Nevertheless, just like the last time he'd made the same assumption, she couldn't help but feel a little flattered. If only his misconceptions of her were true and not a product of the faulty conclusions he'd drawn the night they'd met when she hadn't behaved at all like her normal self.

It would be nice if men had a more exciting view of her, but if her limited experience with them had taught her anything, it was that she didn't inspire their strong emotions. The words the men she was acquainted with used were nice, interesting, intelligent or the one she most detested, comfortable. From her point of view, the words *sedate* and *boring* summed up all her previous relationships and she'd long since given up hope of ever experiencing a "grand passion."

"Well?" Clay prodded irritably, sensing that her mind had drifted away from him. She was the first woman who'd ever gone off on some daydream while in his presence and he didn't like it one bit. "I asked you a question."

"Oh yes, what do I do for excitement?" Carla appeared to give the matter some serious thought. Then she noted the expectant look on his face and she just couldn't seem to help herself. Ignoring the consequences, she surrendered to the same mischievous urge she'd had during their last confrontation. "Actually, I have come across a rather enjoyable pastime lately that's been good for some unexpected laughs, though I sincerely doubt you'd agree."

Clay was pleased that he'd finally accomplished what he'd secretly been hoping for ever since he'd arrived. The prim and proper tax accountant was gone and in her place was the headstrong temptress with the sultry smile and the exotic eyes. Just as it had the last time, the transformation almost took his breath away.

No matter how hard he wished it wasn't so, Clay wanted this woman. "Try me," he challenged.

Her delighted laughter made his heart pound so loudly, he barely heard her response. "What makes this pastime so fascinating is that I'm not sure how much longer I can keep getting away with it. As you know, we intrepid types are always attracted to something that involves a high element of risk."

Clay heard the exhilaration in her voice as she spoke about risk and a cold shiver snaked down his spine. Knowing her background, he could understand why she had this need to go out looking for excitement. Her childhood had been even more restricted than his. Her parents had probably had an attack when she'd rebelled and run off to New York to start her own business. For generations, all the female relatives in her family had sought fulfillment within the confines of a socially acceptable marriage.

According to his sources, Carla's family considered her a renegade who took great joy in reminding them of her association with the only other black sheep in the family, Frederick Valentine. Thumbing her nose at her parents' wishes, she had assumed full financial support of her notorious grandparent. Clay wished he knew how far Carla was willing to go in her rebellion.

Was she tempted to follow in her grandfather's footsteps to strike back at her family? It was obvious that she'd completely rejected their views on moral behavior. Was she just as eager to shun the laws of society?

What if this new occupation of hers involved her in something that was not only slightly illegal but dangerous? Up until this moment, Clay hadn't realized that she inspired more in him than an almost over-whelming lust, but he'd just discovered that he couldn't bear the thought of her getting hurt or being tossed into jail.

"How high?" he demanded tightly.

Carla leaned back in her chair, fluttering her fin-gers in a gesture of confusion. "Baiting bankers? I don't know. You tell me."

Clay made no attempt to hurt her. He didn't leap across the desk, grab her by the throat and squeeze the life out of her as every muscle in his body demanded. He sat perfectly still, fists clenched, and allowed her to calculate the degree of risk she'd just taken.

Very, very high, Carla judged silently, shaken by the effort it took him to restrain himself. It suddenly dawned on her that she was no better judge of char-acter than he was. Clay Chancelor didn't match up with her idea of a wealthy blue-blooded banker any better than she fit his profile of a pragmatic tax ac-countant. Oh, he might dress the part, exude an air of aristocratic refinement and cultured civility, but be-neath his elegant gray suit was a primitive man. The aura of power emanating from him was intrinsic and had absolutely nothing to do with being born with a silver spoon in his mouth.

Clay remained silent until he'd thoroughly con-quered his rage, stunned by how long it took him to do so. Over the years he'd learned to control his emo-tions to a large extent, especially his temper. Violent emotions were a handicap in the investment business. All successful transactions had to be made with a clear head and cold-blooded logic.

Unfortunately, ever since meeting this woman, his blood had run hot and no logic seemed to apply. From the very first, she'd toyed with his emotions as if he were a harmless mouse and she a taunting feline. That deflating analogy brought to mind a recent conversation he'd had with his grandmother. He'd dropped in at her apartment after putting in a grueling, sixteen-hour day at the bank and instead of hearing Lillian commend him for his devotion to business, she'd berated, "If you don't stick your nose out of that vault more often, you're going to become just as lifeless and dull as all those stacks of old money."

Is that why Carla took such joy in provoking him? Did she find him so hopelessly lifeless and dull that she couldn't resist the urge to shake him up? That thought only added to his fury, and the flame in his eyes burned hotter as he glared across the desk at her. "You've been underestimating me, Carla, and if you do it again, I promise you, you'll pay for it."

Carla swallowed hard, sensing that they were about to face off in a brand-new, much more dangerous arena, where she wouldn't be nearly as certain of herself as she had been up until now. He had called her by her first name, establishing an intimacy that she wasn't sure she could handle. Even so, she couldn't seem to stop herself from responding in kind. "I'll take that warning under advisement . . . Clay."

"You do that," he suggested, gratified by the trepidation in her eyes. She wasn't viewing him as a stodgy banker any longer but as a force to be reckoned with, and he planned to make sure that that perception of him didn't change. Until he'd met her, Clay had never experienced feelings of inadequacy; now that he had, he was determined to be equal to whatever was required of him in the future. Right now what was required was a lesson on male superiority.

Slowly, deliberately he focused his eyes on her soft mouth. "Though I doubt the impetuous side of your nature will pay attention to any kind of warning, it'll be interesting to see which facet of your personality wins out in the end—the lady or the vamp."

His gaze drifted lazily down her throat to her voluptuous breasts. "I know which one I'm rooting for."

Carla prayed he didn't hear the note of breathlessness in her voice as she cautioned, "Since you keep seeing a side to my nature that doesn't exist, you're going to be in for a disappointment."

"Maybe."

"Definitely."

Clay shrugged and unfolded his body from the chair. "Then perhaps, I'd better give the vamp a little nudge in the right direction," he said as he strolled around the desk. "I don't deal very well with disappointment."

Carla ordered her body to move as she watched his approach, but got no response. When his hands closed over her shoulders and drew her up from her chair, she stopped thinking altogether. He brought her against him, and she felt hard muscle and steely warmth beneath her cold palms.

It made her aware of the differences between them. Mentally, she could stand up to anything he dished out, but physically, he was bigger and stronger. Oddly, she liked the sensation of being small and fragile in his arms. It made her feel very feminine.

As her fingers flattened helplessly over his shirt-front, Clay's eyes blazed with heat and his breath teased her lips. "But you're not going to disappoint me, are you?"

"Please don't," she pleaded, trembling for the want of something she could never have with this man.

"Do I frighten you, Carla?" he whispered, his mouth hovering over hers, taunting her with forbidden tastes and sinful delights.

"No," she managed weakly and closed her eyes, unable to look without taking. But Clay didn't give her what she wanted. He held his poised position until her lashes lifted up to see why the decision hadn't been taken out of her hands.

Immediately, Carla was aware of the crackling, sensual tension that sizzled between them, nearly palpable in its heated intensity. She stared into Clay's eyes and could feel herself melting.

"You should be frightened," he told her, moving one hand to her throat. "Because you're going to give me something you've never given any other man. Oh, you can try holding back if you need to, but I'm still going to take it. Understand?"

Carla barely had the strength to move her head, but she had to try. Her negative effort brought a punishing response. "Have it your way," Clay ground out just before he took her mouth.

As she felt the intimate invasion of his tongue, Carla forgot to be frightened. As his thrusting tongue began a hot exploration of the inside of her mouth, she forgot everything except the trembling hunger that made her breasts swell against his chest and the blood pound through her veins. A wonderful, aching weakness invaded her body, while at the same time, a pulsing warmth surged to life within her.

She knew that something very important was at stake here, that she shouldn't respond to his kisses, but she didn't make even a token protest. As hard as she'd tried to deny it, this was what she had wanted since she'd first set eyes on him. But not until now had she realized the depth of her need. Her mouth opened to him as her tongue moved to meet his, shyly at first and then with increasing boldness as she tasted the hot spice of passion for the first time.

She loved the taste of him and found she wanted more. She lifted her arms around his neck, tangling her fingers in the silky thickness of his black hair. The inky strands felt cool to her touch, the back of his neck warm. She was overcome by the contrasting textures she discovered as she moved her fingers around to his throat, then upward to the roughness of his jaw. She loved the feel of him almost as much as his taste.

To her surprise, as she emitted a soft murmur of pleasure, Clay seemed to shudder, too. He wrapped his arms around her waist, pulling her even tighter against him. Carla felt the heat and strength of him with every centimeter of her skin and she clenched her fingers in his hair.

"Oh, Clay," she sighed against his mouth. He broke off the kiss, lifting his head a little away from her. His eyes seemed lit by shimmering, raw flames. His answering whisper was hoarse.

"Say that again. Say my name."

If it meant he would kiss her again, she would say anything. "Clay."

"Carla." Her name was a mutter of satisfaction as he lowered his mouth to hers again. Carla clung to him with all her strength, letting him teach her things, then making him the recipient of each new lesson. She had no idea that he wasn't aware of her inexperience, but considered her skilled in the means of seduction he had just taught her himself.

That erroneous assumption prompted him to go beyond kissing. After today she would no longer consider him an old-fashioned prude. He began to undo the tiny pearl buttons of her blouse, continuing to hold her mouth captive with his, while he unfastened her bra with such finesse that Carla was startled to feel his hand cupping her bare breast.

Her first instinct was to pull back, but as he moved his thumb slowly over the sensitive crest, she was overwhelmed by a feverish confusion. Her brain told her that he was going too far, that he had to stop, but another urgency overrode that demand. In a solitary corner of her mind, a joyful voice cried out, *So this is the feeling I've longed for, but never felt. Let it go on forever.*

Clay sensed her resistance and her desire and made certain that desire would win out. He stroked her silky flesh, listened for the quick, indrawing of her breath, then slowly started to remove his hand.

Carla felt the withdrawal of that tingling warmth like a physical pain. Before she could stop herself, she caught his hand and pressed it back. She knew he had to feel the pebble hardness of her nipple against the cupped palm of his hand, but she craved his touch too badly to feel any shame. For once, she would let her senses, not reason, rule her. She would feel what every woman deserved to feel at least once in her life.

In wonder, she felt his mouth leave hers, trace a burning path down her throat to the warm fullness he possessed in his hand. He caught her nipple between his thumb and forefinger, just before closing his lips over the waiting bud. Carla felt a shaft of fire shoot through her body like a thunderbolt. The feeling was wonderful...so wonderful that she gasped in delight.

Clay couldn't remember a time or a woman who had ever created such a need in him by the soft sounds of her pleasure. She liked what he was doing to her so much, he knew he could take her right now if he wanted to, but neither the place nor the situation was right. He swore in silent frustration as he fought the desire to make her his before she realized what had happened.

He ordered his brain not to be affected by a taste so sweet that his mouth refused to give it up. He demanded his mind to take control of his body, which was stubbornly rejecting the slightest move away from her soft, womanly curves. He demanded and ordered but it took several more moments for the commands to get through.

Never had he felt so reluctant to draw away, but he managed it by remembering his original motive for pulling her into his arms. Unfortunately, he was the one who had learned a harsh lesson. With this woman, he'd become less and less a victor and more and more a willing supplicant with each passing second. Her passion entwined him and her beauty bound him to her in ways that he didn't want to analyze, for fear he'd discover that those bonds were unbreakable.

Carla was equally frightened by the revelation she experienced. When Clay lifted his mouth away from her breast, she felt bereft. When he rebuttoned her blouse, she wanted to beg him not to end what had brought her so much pleasure. When she realized how close she'd come to voicing that plea, she was horrified. She couldn't look at him. She would never be able to look him in the face again.

Carla would have been grateful to know that Clay didn't want to face what had just happened between them any more than she did. However, neither of them was forced to deal with the shocking knowledge they'd just learned about themselves and each other. The phone rang and Carla reached across her desk and grabbed for it as if it were a lifeline.

Suffering from the same feeling, Clay headed swiftly for the door. His hand was grasping the knob when he heard her disbelieving groan, "Oh my God." He glanced back and let go of the door. The news she'd just received had to be shocking. He had never seen a more sickly color on any person's face.

Without hesitation, he asked, "What is it, Carla? What's wrong?"

Carla closed her eyes to ward off panic, but the action didn't help. She covered her face in her hands and recited a one word litany that wouldn't change anything. "No...no...no...no."

"Carla!" Clay strode quickly back toward her desk, thinking she might faint. His feelings toward her might be ambivalent, but no matter how badly he needed to get away and sort them out, he couldn't leave her like this.

A second later, he was the one who felt sick as Carla lifted her hands away from her face and informed him, "They've eloped! Freddie and Lillian have eloped!"

Four

―――――

They're at least five hours ahead of us," Clay said, as he shifted his silver Porsche into fifth gear and shot up the entrance ramp to the Long Island Expressway. As soon as he'd maneuvered into the farthest left lane, he cast a killing glance at the woman who occupied the black leather seat next to his. "More than enough time to tie the knot, wouldn't you say?"

Carla glanced at her watch, mentally tabulating the time it would have taken her grandfather to rent a car, drive to Connecticut and get married. According to the resident manager at Ridgeport, Freddie and Lillian had left the retirement complex at three p.m. If traffic on the expressway was as heavy as usual, it would have taken several hours for them to get off the island, cross the East River into the Bronx and drive north across the state line.

It was now half past eight and going by Carla's calculations, the elderly couple wouldn't have arrived at their destination too much earlier. "Normal business hours are over. The chapel could be closed."

Clay snorted in disgust. "Dream on, lady. Wiley's Wedding Chapel doesn't sound like a nine-to-five operation to me."

"You don't know that," Carla argued. "Besides, even if they normally stay open day and night, we could still be in luck. Some of those places only operate in the summer months and this is still the off-season."

Clay grunted his response to that hope and Carla immediately dropped the subject. He'd been acting like a Neanderthal ever since she'd gotten that phone call from George Byers and she had the bruises to show for it. Gazing down at her reddened wrist, she wondered how she could ever have judged this man as civilized.

Clay shot her another glance in order to see if she'd finally accepted reality. At first, he was gratified by the sight of her downcast head, but then he saw what she was looking at. The marks on her arm reminded him that no matter how tough she tried to appear on the outside, she was a very small, very delicate woman. He tightened his lips grimly. "Did I do that?"

"Of course not," Carla negated tartly. "You're much too well-mannered a person to drag an unwilling woman down three flights of stairs because you couldn't wait for the elevator."

Taking perverse pleasure in his guilty flush, Carla lifted the hem of her black plaid skirt to reveal the unbecoming snags in her black-textured hose. "And such a fine gentleman as you would never have thrust a lady into the seat of his car without bothering to make sure her legs were clear of the door."

Through the spreading gap of nylon over her knee, Clay could see an inch-long scratch. His face got even redder. "Why didn't you say something?"

"As I recall," Carla sniffed, "when this happened, you were verbally contemplating the most violent means to murder my grandfather and I didn't want to risk having my name added to your hit list."

Jaw clenched, Clay muttered, "You know damned well that I'm not going to murder anybody."

"Hmmm," Carla mused consideringly. "Then when you vowed to smash my grandfather's face into a pulp after wringing his neck, you weren't expecting him to die as a result. Your high moral principles wouldn't allow you to murder an old man, only torture him right?"

"I'm not going to torture him, either!"

"Oh, I see," Carla persisted, not knowing what compelled her to provoke him, but unable to stop herself from doing it. "Roughing up his granddaughter has temporarily satisfied your need for vengeance."

"Roughing up his...?" Clay's mouth snapped shut as he caught sight of the contrary gleam in her eyes. She was needling him like this on purpose. Just like all the other times, she was planning to sit back and enjoy herself while he made a fool out of himself. Only this time, he wasn't going to let her get away with it.

"Well, there's an idea I hadn't thought of," he admitted, letting his expression show that he was deriving a great deal of pleasure from thinking about it now. "If we're too late to stop the dirty deed, I could take out my revenge on your beautiful body. I could act on the urge I've had to pull all those pins from your hair and capture its fire in my hands. I could even...hmmm. Why not?"

Clay checked the rearview mirror and switched lanes. He slowed down to match the other traffic, then switched over to the right again. A few moments later, the Porsche was traveling well below the speed limit in bumper-to-bumper traffic in a lane that would soon branch off onto another expressway.

"What on earth are you doing?" Carla inquired warily.

"I'm turning back."

"You are not."

"Yes, I am," Clay replied smoothly. "I've just decided that if I stop this marriage, I won't get my pound of flesh from the person I'd most like to get it from."

"You've decided no such thing," Carla stated firmly, but they were coming closer and closer to the exit and he wasn't making any attempt to switch out of the lane. "You can't be serious!"

"You forget that I've already had a sample of your charms, Carla," he announced with a fanatical gleam in his eye, gratified by her fiery blush. "Since the odds of our catching up with your grandfather before he makes everything legal are slim to none, I'd be crazy to turn down this chance to enjoy more than just a taste of you. Even as we speak, the bird in the bush is getting away, but I have no intention of losing the bird in the hand until I've stroked a few of her fine feathers.''

Carla was certain he was only baiting her. Well, she wasn't going to swallow the bait even if his suggestive words made her eyes pop out and her mouth gape like that of a fish. All she had to do was be patient and wait until they reached the point where there was no turning back.

They reached it. The Porsche shot forward as they passed it and merged onto the new highway. Carla was no longer sure of anything. ''Barclay Northrop Chancelor, you turn this car around right now, or I'll . . . I'll . . .''

Leering over at her, Clay drawled, ''You'll what? Scream? Who would hear you? Of course, you can scream all you want when I've got you in bed. It will only add to my pleasure.''

Carla grabbed for the door handle but Clay pressed down on the automatic lock before she could open it. ''Don't you dare try that again!''

Carla took one look at his face and quickly subsided back in her seat. ''I . . . I won't.''

Clay took a deep breath and tried to calm down. He'd intended to give her a dose of her own medicine and show her what kind of trouble she was asking for if she made a practice of provoking strange men, but he'd never expected her to throw herself out of a moving car! If he didn't know better, he would assume that she considered the prospect of his making love to her as a fate worse than death.

Knowing how her devious mind worked, that was exactly what she'd wanted him to think and she'd also wanted to scare the life out of him. She was the most irritating woman he'd ever met and one who took far too many chances. She'd known all along that he would stop her from opening the door, but if his reflexes had been just a few seconds slower....

"Are you crazy? You could've gotten yourself killed pulling a stupid stunt like that!"

Carla pressed herself against the door, placing as much distance between them as she possibly could. She was in the clutches of a madman and he was asking her if *she* was crazy? A shiver of fear rippled down her spine.

Fear changed to terror as she remembered the strength she'd felt beneath her fingers earlier today when he'd kissed her, the steel in his arms as they'd pulled her against him. She knew he was strong and handsome and rich but what else did she really know about this man? Just because he was gorgeous and could buy and sell most people, didn't mean he couldn't have a dark side to his nature.

She'd been witness to his violent temper, heard him talk with an almost fiendish relish about murder and torture. What proof did she have that he wasn't truly planning to take her off to god-knows-where and do god-knows-what to her defenseless body? Would a normal person threaten a woman like this?

Upon answering these questions, Carla pleaded brokenly, her eyes brimming with anxious tears. "Please don't hurt me."

Hearing the genuine fear in her voice, Clay's mouth dropped open in shock. He looked at her and knew that she wasn't faking the emotion. She actually considered him capable of...? This was no longer funny. "Carla, calm down. I was only teasing."

He could tell by her face that she didn't believe him and that hit him where it hurt. She'd badly misjudged his character several times in their short acquaintance, but this defamation was too much. He would never force a woman to do anything against her will.

He was a highly respected businessman who came from a socially prominent, upstanding family. Other than a few speeding tickets, he'd never broken a single law. Yet this idiotic woman assumed he was another Jack the Ripper. "Don't look at me like that!"

Carla flinched in terror at the cutting edge to his voice. "I'm sorry."

Clay watched the tears spill over onto her pale cheeks and cursed himself ten times over. If there'd been any place to pull off the road, he would have done so immediately, but there wasn't even a shoulder. He had a semihysterical woman on his hands. He was to blame for her overwrought state and there wasn't anything he could do about it but make an illegal U-turn on two wheels, then speed down the expressway in the opposite direction.

He was back on the expressway before Carla found the courage to open her eyes and peek out the windshield. Even then, she wasn't quite sure what this latest maneuver meant and she didn't dare ask. The look on his face was much too forbidding.

"Let's get something straight right now," Clay said once he'd safely guided the car into the fast lane. "I don't know what kind of brutal men you're used to dealing with, but I'm a very nice person!"

Carla nodded obediently though her eyes told him that she would agree with whatever he said if it would prevent him from becoming violent.

Clay scowled at her. "Look lady, you've taken great pleasure in making me the butt of your private little jokes ever since we met, yet when I try to get some of my own back, you make me out as some sort of madman."

"Oh, no. I don't think you're mad. Really," Carla hastened to assure him, still keeping her body as far away from him as she could.

"Dammit, Carla!" Clay hit the steering wheel with his open palm. "You're not playing fair. Just because I'm a man and you're a woman, am I supposed to sit back and take whatever you care to dish out? I've got feelings too, you know."

Carla was astonished by the indignation in his voice and the hurt expression on his face. Anyone, even a terrified wimp of a woman, could see that both of these feelings were real. "I don't think I understand what you're trying to tell me."

"I'm trying to say that I'm sorry for scaring you," Clay said. "I never dreamed you'd take me so seriously. Or maybe I did . . . I don't know. For some reason, you bring out my baser instincts."

He shook his head as if he didn't understand his recent behavior any better than she did. "I don't know why, but whenever I'm around you, I find myself saying and doing crazy things, things I've never said or done to any woman in my life."

Since Carla suffered from the same problem around him, she could readily sympathize. All she had to do was be in the same room with him and she turned into an entirely different person. Looking at him, there could be no doubt that he was suffering from the same baffling ailment. "Since I'm rarely myself around you either, I guess I shouldn't hold that against you."

"I'd appreciate it if you didn't," Clay said sincerely. The last thing he wanted was for her to be afraid of him. Respect him yes, but not fear him. But until they'd successfully stopped their grandparents' wedding, he couldn't act on his initial impulse to take her to bed. However, he could smooth the way for that inevitable moment when they made love.

"We're both on edge, Carla, and with good reason," he said. "I'll try not to make it worse for you, if you're willing to do the same by me. Okay?"

"Okay." Carla pulled herself away from the door and relaxed back in the plush leather seat. She smiled faintly. "At least, I can promise to try."

"I can't ask for more than that." In one of the most friendly overtures he'd ever made toward her, Clay reached across the space between them to take her hand. Then, before he grasped hold of her fingers, he realized that she might view the gesture as another threat and quickly pulled back his arm.

"Sorry," he muttered as he wrapped his offending fingers around the gearshift. "You've made it quite clear that you'd rather jump out of the car than have me touch you."

The hurt was back in his voice and Carla had the surprising urge to make amends to him despite the circumstances. She might have given him a good deal of grief lately, but his method of evening the score was despicable. He had prayed upon one of a woman's worst fears. It was lucky for him that the relief she felt outweighed her darker emotions.

"I was scared and I overreacted," she allowed. "It seems that I have a very active imagination."

"Is that what it was?" Clay asked, his brow deeply furrowed. "Or have you been in similar circumstances before? Have you . . . has some man hurt you, Carla?"

Carla could understand why he would prefer to hear that she'd behaved as she had because she'd been reliving some horrible experience from her past. Unfortunately, she couldn't lie about something like that just to soothe his wounded ego. However, she could assure him that she would never jump to such an erroneous conclusion about him again. "No, I've never been assaulted, but most women live with the fear. I'm sorry for thinking you could be that cruel. I know better now."

A huge knot untangled in Clay's stomach as Carla reached between the seats and placed her hand over his on the gearshift. But it tightened up again as she said, "You might have a terrible temper, a lousy disposition and a rotten sense of humor, but you're not a monster."

"Thanks," he stated gruffly, not sure whether to be grateful for the vote of confidence or angry at the insults.

Carla patted his hand, offered him a lovely smile and Clay opted for grateful. "You're not so bad either," he conceded graciously. "Even if you do provoke my easygoing temper, dampen my sunny disposition and spoil my good humor."

"Thanks," Carla replied with an indignant little sniff and promptly returned her hand to her lap.

Clay chuckled and pressed down on the accelerator. "Don't worry. If you turn out to be right and the wedding chapel's closed, we might not have a problem. My grandmother never stays up past eight o'clock. If they didn't get married, I'll find her in the nearest hotel."

"And if I'm wrong?"

"Then you can hold down the justice of the peace while I convince him to annul the marriage."

Carla nodded. "That sounds fair."

They rode along in an amazingly companionable silence for several more miles until Carla had an awful thought. "Oh, no. Why didn't I think of this before?"

"Think of what?"

"There's a very good chance that Freddie left behind that clue for us to find just so we'd go off in the wrong direction," Carla fretted. "My grandfather has a very devious mind."

"He couldn't know that George would call you and we'd find out about his plans," Clay reminded her, refusing to think about the possibility that she could be right.

Carla fished in her purse for the folded piece of scratch paper she'd discovered next to the phone in

Freddie's apartment. "Wiley's Wedding Chapel," she mused thoughtfully. "Isn't that name just a bit too appropriate? A Wiley wedding for a wily man?"

"The place exists," Clay insisted. "And the rental agent assured us that the car was being dropped off in Lockeford, Connecticut. That's where they're heading all right."

"I wouldn't be too sure," Carla cautioned. "It would be just like Freddie to leave a false trail."

"Dammit!" Clay bit out in frustration. "If he has ... I swear, when I get my hands on that cunning old con artist, I'm going to tear him—"

"Please don't start that again," Carla pleaded wearily. "He is my grandfather and I happen to love him. He's not really a bad person, Clay. He just has a different set of priorities than other people."

"And right now, my innocent grandmother is the focus of those misguided priorities," Clay reminded her. "Frankly, I don't care whose grandfather he is or who loves him. Lillian Chancelor is the sweetest, most generous woman in the world and protecting her from a broken heart is the only thing I care about. If that old man hurts her in any way, shape or form, I'll make him wish he was never born. I'll—"

"If you harm one hair on my grandfather's head, I'll make sure you wish the same thing!" Carla broke in before he could launch into another of his tirades.

"Oh yeah? You and who else?"

"Me and nobody else!"

"I'm quaking in my boots, Ms. Valentine," Clay taunted, his temper dying at the thought of them going at each other one on one. The woman barely came up to his shoulder and wringing wet, she would probably tip the scales at less than a hundred-and-ten pounds. He had over sixty pounds on her.

Lips twitching, he pictured her stepping into the ring with him at Madison Square Garden. Like him, she would be wearing nothing but a huge pair of satin boxer shorts. She would need both hands to keep them from falling down around her ankles. Then, she would put up her dukes and it would all be over. Gentleman that he was, he would do his best to protect her modesty, but....

Clay let out an appreciative chuckle. Around the world, boxing fans would call it the contest of the century, even more memorable than the thriller in Manila.

"What's so funny!" Carla burst out, certain she'd been assigned a starring role in whatever X-rated comedy he was acting out in his mind.

Reluctantly, Clay cleared his head of a most enjoyable picture. "Believe me, honey, you wouldn't like to know what I was thinking."

"I don't like being called honey, either, but that hasn't stopped you from doing it."

"That's true." Clay grinned unrepentantly and refused to elaborate any further.

"You've got to be the most irritating man in the world," Carla grumbled. "The most rude, overbearing and obnoxious male it has ever been my misfortune to meet."

Clay couldn't remember when he'd ever been so pleased by a litany of disparaging remarks. It was nice to know that he was as upsetting to her as she was to him. Perhaps the little rebel had finally realized that he couldn't be counted on to think and behave like other well-bred members of his class.

His investigation of her background had uncovered the information that while she was growing up, her family had only allowed her to associate with young men from the most prominent families in Boston society. From personal experience, Clay knew that many of these supposedly elite individuals would bore an intelligent woman like Carla to death. No wonder she'd run off in search of more exciting members of the male species.

Hopefully, he'd just shown her that she'd found one. In better spirits than he'd been in all day, Clay observed pleasantly, "It looks like we've both got to try harder to stick to our truce until we find out whether or not we're related by marriage."

Carla rolled her eyes. "Now there's a sickening thought."

Clay caught himself before reacting to the gibe. "Do we have a deal or not?"

"Deal," Carla agreed.

To keep to the agreement, neither of them dared say much of anything as they covered the distance to Connecticut. They commented about the seasonably warm weather, the horrendous traffic on I95 and the beauty of their surroundings as they cut away from the interstate onto a winding, tree-lined road that would eventually take them to the small village of Lockeford.

It was almost midnight by the time they finally located Wiley's Wedding Chapel. It would have been much later if they hadn't stopped to get specific directions at a local gas station. Without them, they might have searched for the hidden turn off the main road all night.

Situated at the end of a narrow, private driveway running parallel to a steep woodland ravine, Wiley's reminded Carla of a picturesque country inn. The three-story colonial-style building stood in the center of at least five acres of beautifully landscaped lawns, well-kept gardens and tall, stately trees. At the front of the multiwindowed structure was a grassy courtyard that housed a free-standing wooden swing, wicker lawn chairs and a variety of flowering shrubs. The courtyard was lit by the golden glow from several strategically placed lampposts and enclosed by a quaint white picket fence.

"Just look at this place," Carla murmured in awe.

"Evidently, the wedding business brings in a sizable profit," Clay muttered, counting the number of cars that were parked along the circular driveway. "And they're doing a lively business tonight by the looks of it."

"Yes it does," Carla agreed.

Every window in the entire building was lit up and the place was enormous. Carla counted six chimneys and eight pediments jutting out from the black slanted roof. She could just imagine the handsome staircases, lofty ceilings and ornate plasterwork that were likely to be found inside.

"Are you sure this is the right place?"

Clay pointed through the windshield at the neatly lettered wooden sign hanging from the nearby gatepost and read out loud, ''Wiley's Wedding Chapel, William Wiley, J.P....'' He reached down and turned off the ignition. ''I'll say this much for the old man. He couldn't have found a more out of the way location.''

''Nor one more charming and romantic,'' Carla replied softly, noting another even smaller sign that announced the availability of rented rooms. ''Any woman would adore the thought of getting married and spending their honeymoon in a place like this.''

''Come on,'' Clay growled, annoyed by the dreamy expression on her face. ''Let's find out if my grandmother adored more than just the thought.''

Five

Standing before the front doors of the imposing colonial structure, Carla read the motto carved into the portico and reached the same conclusion she'd arrived at hours earlier. Considering his personality, Frederick Valentine couldn't have chosen a more fitting place to get married. The words, "Jollity, the offspring of wisdom and good living" described his philosophy of life to perfection.

Actually, Carla thought both the name and the place and its motto seemed just a tad too perfect. She had heard her crafty grandfather express this same sentiment many times over in the last two years, but never more adamantly than when he was trying to convince her to ascribe to this philosophy. She could almost hear his voice telling her that the best days of her life were slipping away while she holed up in a stuffy office with her nose buried in an accounting ledger. How could she be happy with no romance, no pleasure and no time off for fun?

Carla felt an odd, prickling sensation at the back of her neck as she recalled Freddie's words and was reminded of the various other times in the last several hours that she'd experienced this same sense of unease. The first time was when Freddie's neighbor, George Byers had called to tell her about the elopement. As far as she knew, George had stopped speaking to Freddie the night he'd lost money to him in a fixed game of craps.

Clay had grabbed the phone out of her hand before she'd been able to question George any further, but now she would dearly like to know why a man, who supposedly wanted nothing further to do with his underhanded neighbor, would call her up and plead with her to stop his "good friend" from making an irrevocable mistake. Then, when she'd arrived in answer to his call, "concerned" George had been nowhere to be found.

The next time she'd felt a niggle of apprehension was when the man at the car rental agency had revealed that he knew the whereabouts of Wiley's Wedding Chapel. She had thought it an odd coincidence that said agent's niece had run off and gotten married at the very same place just three months before. And then, there was that gas station attendant in Lockeford who had been so surprised to hear that "old man Wiley" was no longer retired. As far as he knew, the chapel had been closed down for several years.

Yet, according to all the cars parked along the circular driveway and all the lights on in the building, the resident justice of the peace was still doing a booming business. Why would the locals be unaware of this apparently thriving concern?

Carla couldn't get over the feeling that something was rotten in the state of Denmark. She didn't have anything concrete to go on, but the suspicion refused to go away. As she watched Clay lift the heavy brass knocker on the chapel's front doors, she offered a silent prayer that whatever scheme her grandfather had gotten her involved in this time would not result in her having to be fitted for a straitjacket.

Neither Carla nor Clay were prepared for the greeting they received from the birdlike old woman with scraggly orange hair who opened the door to them. Peering down at the gold watch she had pinned to the sagging bodice of her blue flannel bathrobe, she shook a finger at them. "Why can't you young people ever wait until a decent hour to come calling? You might not mind getting married in the middle of the night, but me and the mister need our rest, don't you know?"

Before they had a chance to respond to her testy questions, she stepped forward and wrapped her bony fingers around Carla's arm. "Well, don't just stand there. Come on in. I'm not waking Will, but that don't mean I'll refuse you a room. Nowadays, it don't matter to folks if you have your wedding night before the ceremony. Young man, you can go back out and get your luggage."

Clay stifled a chuckle as Carla hurried to correct the woman's misconceptions. "We're not here to get married. All we want is to speak with the justice of the peace, Mrs...?"

"Wiley, didn't you see the sign?"

"Yes, of course, Mrs. Wiley," Carla said, glowering over her shoulder at Clay as the amazingly strong little woman pulled her across the threshold and into a brightly lit center hall.

"I'd rather you call me Lucille. I'll be the witness at your wedding and it seems so unfriendly not to be on a first name basis with the person who stands up for you, don't you know?"

Carla heard the bark of laughter behind her, but her deceptively fragile-looking captor didn't allow her to stop long enough to launch a hard backward kick to Clay's shin. "It's very nice meeting you, Lucille. My name is Carla Valentine and this is Clay Chancelor. Do either of those names sound familiar to you?"

"Sure," the woman replied cheerfully as she came to a stop at the end of the long hallway and finally let go of Carla's arm. "Just let me step behind the desk and get the register."

She disappeared for a moment in back of the wide mahogany enclosure that looked like the registration desk in any ordinary hotel, then popped back up, holding a heavy, leather-bound book in her skinny arms. Plunking down the guest book on the desk's gleaming surface, she offered generously, "I won't mind if you sign with your married name. First thing in the morning it'll all be legal anyway. Nice name for a couple, Carla and Clay Valentine."

"It would be Chancelor," Carla corrected, before she realized what she was saying. She didn't dare look at Clay, knowing she would turn a blistering shade of red if she saw the mocking grin that had to be on his face.

Lucille's disapproving snort reclaimed Carla's attention. "Can't say I approve of the man taking the woman's name, but then, if he don't mind, who am I to complain? Still, don't you think there's going to be a whole lot of unnecessary confusion when you two start having babies?"

"There's no need to discuss our having children," Clay reminded the woman, stepping up beside Carla who was beginning to look slightly frazzled.

"Oh, I see." Lucille wrinkled up her tiny nose and her gray eyes appeared sad. "You're one of those real modern couples who've decided against having children."

"We haven't decided anything—" Clay began, then stopped himself when he noted the gleeful expression on Carla's face. He'd been right on the verge of getting into the same kind of trouble with this obtuse little woman as she had.

"Lucille," he started over. "All we need are the answers to a few questions. Earlier, you said that you recognized our names? Why is that?"

"Sure I recognize them," Lucille replied, tilting her head to one side as if she were hoping that gravity might help her dislodge some vital piece of information from the depths of her clogged brain.

As the seconds ticked on, both Clay and Carla found themselves leaning forward, anticipating the moment when Lucille would divulge the words they hoped to hear. It was amazing that neither of them groaned in frustration when the woman finally recalled what she wanted to say. "I'd estimate that over the last fifty years, we've probably married twenty Carlas and at least six or seven Clays. Those names really aren't that uncommon, you know. We've only had one Aloysius. Now there's a name you don't hear often anymore. And then there's Valonia. Ever heard of a name like Valonia?"

Clay cracked under the strain. "Mrs. Wiley!"

Shaking her head, Carla placed her hand on Clay's sleeve. "Let me give it another try."

Clay turned his hands over palms up. "Be my guest."

"Lucille," Carla began, speaking very slowly and clearly. "Mr. Chancelor and I would like to find out if you were a witness for our grandparents today, Frederick Valentine and Lillian Chancelor? We have reason to believe that they came here this afternoon to get married."

"Your grandparents!" Lucille's wispy white eyebrows went up. "You mean they've just been living together up till now? People their age?"

"Can I be of some help here?"

Clay and Carla turned around to face the owner of that deep, bass voice. He was an older man, probably in his early seventies, but he cut an imposing figure even in his gray flannel pajamas and red woolen robe. Over six feet tall, his back was ramrod straight and his shoulders impressively broad. He had a full head of silver hair, a rakish handlebar mustache and sharp blue eyes. "I'm William Wiley."

Clay pumped the man's outstretched hand with far more vigor than the introduction warranted, grateful for any outside offer of assistance. "You're the justice of the peace, correct?"

"That's right. How may I help you young people?"

Before either Clay or Carla had the chance to open their mouths, Lucille began speaking to her husband in a tone that left them both momentarily speechless. "You've no business being out of bed, sweetie," she cooed, her pale lips pouting. "I can handle this little matter. You need your rest after such a busy day."

In an aside to Carla and Clay, she murmured, "He's such a darling and never complains, but he's had a bad throat all week, don't you know?"

"I'm sorry to hear that you're not feeling well, Mr. Wiley, and we'll try to take up very little of your time," Clay put in hastily, just in case the man took his wife's advice and went back to bed before they found out anything.

Carla had the same thought and was just as anxious in her appeal. "Mr. Wiley, can you tell us if you performed a marriage for Frederick Valentine and Lillian Chancelor today? We're their grandchildren and we really need to find them. We have urgent family business to discuss."

Wiley turned to his wife and gave her a loving smile before saying, "Yes, they stopped by here earlier, around seven-thirty, but Lucy never lets me work after supper. She wouldn't let me perform the ceremony so they left.''

"Thank God," Carla breathed, sagging with relief. Only seconds ago, she'd wanted to strangle Lucille Wiley, but now she would like to give her a huge hug.

Clay wasn't as quick to believe that their problem had been solved so easily. "Did they say where they were going after they left here?"

Wiley thought for a moment, then stated, "I believe they were planning to take a room in town and come back out in the morning. I don't know why they didn't want to stay here tonight, but Mr. Valentine said something about requiring more privacy."

"As if any place could be more private than this," Lucille harrumphed. "I told them that they wouldn't get the kind of personal service at Howard Johnson's that we provide for all our guests, but they insisted that they'd rather stay someplace else. No accountin' for people's tastes, don't you know?"

"Can you direct us there?" Clay asked the woman's husband.

Wiley stepped up to the desk. "Would you hand me a pen and some paper, dear? It would be easier if I drew them a map."

"Won't you let me take care of this for you, snook-ums? I can get them over to the Holiday Inn as good as anyone," Lucille declared petulantly, as she opened a drawer and pulled out a pad of paper. "You do far too much around here, William."

Carla hoped the woman didn't hear her and Clay's collective sigh of relief as Wiley said, "It's all right, Lucy. This'll only take a moment."

The man was true to his word and less than five minutes later, Carla and Clay were back inside the car. Clay thrust the key into the ignition, then turned to face her. "I don't think I've ever met a more mismatched couple. What could an intelligent man like him possibly see in that lamebrained woman?"

"I thought their relationship was rather sweet," Carla retorted. "Besides, maybe she's getting a little senile. If that happens to me in my old age, I hope I'll have a husband who's as loving and patient as William Wiley. And it sounds as if Lucy takes very good care of him, too. If you recall, she won't let him work after supper in case he gets too tired."

Clay snorted. "She sounded more like his mother than his wife."

"Not really," Carla disagreed. "Her eyes lit up and her voice went all soft as soon as he came into the room. I'd bet you anything that they've got a very romantic relationship. They've both got to be over seventy, yet she was batting her eyelashes as if she were a girl of sixteen."

"What eyelashes?" Clay inquired heartlessly. "Of course, I was so distracted by the clacking of her false teeth, I might have missed seeing them."

"But Will didn't," Carla said. "His eyes never left her face."

"Forget what I said earlier. The man must be a total idiot."

Carla laughed. "There's no accountin' for tastes, snookums, don't you know?"

Picturing Carla as an old woman, Clay amazed himself with the thought that he would probably want her at any age. Her kind of sexiness was an inherent thing, having nothing to do with age. The classic lines of her face wouldn't suffer from the ravages of time, The exotic slant to her eyes was eternal and he couldn't imagine a time when he wouldn't want to kiss the pouty fullness of her lower lip.

Maybe William Wiley had experienced the same thoughts about his Lucille fifty years earlier. "Now there's a humbling notion," he muttered to himself as he turned the key in the ignition.

"What is?" Carla wanted to know, but moved on to another question when she heard the engine grinding with no result. "What's the matter?"

"What does it sound like?"

"It sounds like the car won't start."

"Smart deduction," Clay commented dryly, attempted to turn over the engine once more, then gave up after slamming his fist against the steering wheel.

Carla gave him what she thought was a commendable amount of time to recover, but when after several moments, he made no move to get out of the car, she prompted, "Shouldn't we go look under the hood?"

"What for?" Clay asked, his jaw appearing even more marble-like than usual.

"How should I know what for?" Carla didn't know the first thing about cars and even less about foreign ones, but Clay was a man, surely he'd picked up at least a smattering of mechanical knowledge along the way to adulthood. She was certain that a working knowledge of the combustion engine was considered one of the classic rites of manhood, even for the very rich.

When Clay continued doing nothing but malign the character of the car's engine, Carla made what she thought was a perfectly reasonable suggestion. "Swearing at it won't get us anywhere. Just go out and find whatever doohicky is responsible for starting this thing."

Clay gave her a look that would have prompted a lesser woman to turn tail and run. He spoke through clenched teeth. "The reason I'm swearing, Ms. Valentine, is because I wouldn't know a doohicky from a thingamajig. I'd take it very kindly if you would get off my case so I can continue doing the only thing I know how to do when my car breaks down. Over the years, I've developed a string of profanity and I don't care to be interrupted until I've made use of every word."

Carla sucked in her lips to keep from laughing as he proceeded to do just that. When silence reigned once more, she inquired gently, "Feel better now?"

"Much better," Clay admitted and even managed a sheepish smile. "Let's go inside and see how Lucille plans to handle this problem."

Carla groaned at the prospect, but was right behind him when they retraced their steps to the front doors. "Don't fight it when she hauls you inside," she advised him. "If you go willingly, her steely talons will only hurt for the first three feet or so."

The doors opened before Clay got his hand on the brass knocker. "I've put you in 208," Lucille announced without preamble as she dragged Clay inside. "We'll call Jed in the morning. Won't do a speck of good to call him tonight."

"Who's Jed?" Carla asked, trying to keep pace with Lucille who was marching Clay towards the registration desk.

"The only mechanic in town who'll work on them fancy foreign cars," Lucille told her just before she dropped Clay's arm and ducked behind the desk. Thrusting a pen out to Clay, she added, "And he's also the only one willing to come out here, but he won't come out at night. Every business in Lockeford is closed up by now."

It didn't dawn on Carla that Clay was actually planning to spend the night until she saw him sign the register. "We can't stay here."

"I don't see that we've got much choice," Clay said, as he handed her the pen. "It's going on one a.m. and it's been a hellish day. We don't have a car and I for one am dog tired. Besides, with our kind of luck, we'll have twice the chance of meeting up with the grandfolks when they come back tomorrow, than we would trying to catch up with them tonight."

"But Clay—"

"Come on now, honey." Lucille cut off Carla's objections with a wave of her hand. "Your man is tired. You don't expect him to walk all those miles back to town when I just told you there won't be anyone there to help."

"Of course I don't expect him to do that. I just meant that we could at least try and call someone," Carla said, forgetting how this woman's mind worked.

To her consternation, the words were considered an acknowledgment of Clay's position in her life.

Giving Carla an approving smile, she handed Clay a room key. "I'll get on to Sam first thing in the morning. He's the best mechanic you're ever going to find," she assured. "Now you two go right on up to bed and don't give this trouble any more thought."

Carla glanced at Clay to make sure he'd noticed that their mechanic had undergone a name change. He had, but neither one of them dared to question Lucille about it. They still hadn't recovered from the last time they'd entered a discussion with her concerning names. Even so, Carla's surrender to the inevitable wasn't gracious. "Oh all right, we'll spend the night."

"Up those stairs and to the left," Lucille directed.

"We'll require a second room," Carla insisted firmly.

"All booked up except for 208," Lucille declared with finality as she closed the guest book and turned off the light over the desk. "You can pay me in the morning. I'm sure you're an honest couple and I don't have a head for finances this late at night, don't you know?"

Carla sighed and gave up. Clay averted his face so she wouldn't see how pleased he was by the prospect of sharing a room with her. Not ten seconds later, Lucille scooted out from behind the desk and shut off the rest of the lights in the hall. "Goodnight now and sleep well," she called back over her shoulder as she disappeared through a swinging door to the right of the staircase.

Clay groped for Carla's hand in the darkness and luckily they made it to the bottom step without bumping into anything. "The lights on the second floor are still on, but I have the feeling we'd better find our room in a hurry. Lucille is closing up for the night."

"I don't believe that woman," Carla muttered darkly as Clay pulled her up the stairs.

Lucille Wiley waited in the kitchen until she heard footsteps on the second floor and the sound of a door closing. Then she walked down the back hallway and entered the private study situated at the rear of the house. Three people were seated before the fireplace, gazing into the cheery fire and drinking brandy. Lucille picked up the glass they had poured for her and sat down in the wing chair next to the one occupied by her husband.

"They make a splendid couple. Don't you think so, Will?"

"If I didn't, I'd never have touched that complicated engine," William Wiley said, slipping his hand inside the pocket of his robe and pulling out several small metal pieces. "Whatever these are, they must be necessary for the efficient running of a Porsche."

The man seated on the couch nodded his appreciation. "Well done, Willie my boy, well done."

The woman seated next to him wasn't as quick to bestow her commendations. "Clay didn't suspect anything did he?"

"Believe me," Lucille declared with a merry laugh, "I confused and frustrated them so badly that they didn't dare to ask me any more questions for fear I might answer."

William chuckled. "I often suffer from the same problem around you, darling."

Lucille smiled. "Why Will, what a sweet thing to say."

All three of her companions laughed at that. Basking in their approval, Lucille took a sip of her brandy. "Anyone up for a game of three-card monte? I feel very lucky tonight."

William sighed, "Careful friends. After fifty years of marriage, I still can't catch her sleight of hand. I've warned her what will happen if I ever do, but she's got the magic touch."

Pulling off her scraggly wig, Lucille lifted her glass to the ceiling and offered a toast, "May the young woman upstairs always have the same good fortune."

William swiftly followed with a toast of his own. "And may the young man never tire of catching her magic."

The couple on the couch lifted their glasses and pronounced, "Hear! hear!"

Six

Carla knew she would have to come out of the bathroom eventually, but after twenty minutes, she still wasn't ready to face what she knew was waiting for her on the other side of the locked door. How did I get myself into this mess? she asked herself miserably and as usual, the smiling visage of a silver-haired rascal came into her head. Frederick Valentine felt it was his duty to bring some excitement into her boring life, but this time he'd gone too far.

Due to his latest scam, she'd had to endure verbal abuse, severe mental torture and even a certain amount of bodily harm at the hands of a man who was now expecting her to join him beneath the canopy of a huge four-poster bed. Carla's erstwhile grandparent had a lot to answer for. Throughout the entire day, she'd comforted herself with the picture of what she was going to say and do to Freddie the minute she caught up with him.

As much satisfaction as that picture had given her, however, it wasn't going to help her get through the night. Sooner or later, she was going to have to deal with the fact that she was staying in the same room with a man who assumed she was the kind of woman who slipped in and out of strange beds all the time. Worse than that, she didn't trust her ability to prove otherwise.

Around Clay, she couldn't seem to restrain any of the emotions she'd restrained all her life. Her temper rose and fell like a barometer responding to the erratic changes in an increasingly more volatile atmosphere. Her female passions were so close to the surface, that a simple touch, the mere sound of Clay's voice, made her nerve endings tingle with a sweet, yearning fire. Every part of her body was oversensitized by him with an awareness so acute it was becoming painful.

I'm the world's oldest living virgin by choice and that choice remains mine, no matter what Clay says or does, she reminded herself a bit desperately, as she studied her reflection in the wide mirror over the vanity.

As she expected, her pink silk teddy left very little to the imagination, and Carla feared that as soon as Clay saw her in it, he would leap to some very wrong conclusions. More unsettling was the knowledge that when she climbed into that bed with him, the distance separating them would be negligible.

Even so, she couldn't sleep in her clothes. If she came back into the room still fully clothed when it had supposedly taken her close to a half hour to prepare for bed, Clay would laugh so hard, he would probably fall off the mattress. Striving to see what Clay would see when he looked at her, Carla studied her reflection with critical eyes, then frowned at her conclusion. The woman staring back at her might look like a mature, sophisticated woman of twenty-seven, capable of handling any situation with panache, but she felt like a wide-eyed innocent, tongue-tied and awkward over the possibility of being half-naked in bed with an equally half-naked man.

Or maybe by now he was all naked. Gorgeous and naked. Gorgeous and naked . . . and aroused.

"Are you *ever* coming out of there?"

Carla jumped at the sound of Clay's voice, stubbing her toe on the clawfoot tub. Her outcry brought an even more disturbing response from her roommate.

Clay pounded on the door and demanded, "Carla, are you okay?"

"I'm fine," she told him through clenched teeth. "Go back to bed. I'll be out in a minute. I just have to . . . um . . . remove the rest of my makeup."

Clay had the ill grace to call her on the lie. "You weren't wearing any makeup when you went in there."

Carla made nasty faces at the door, but her tone was even as she insisted, "Any cosmetician can tell you that the best artifice is the kind that doesn't show."

"Right," Clay grunted, but to Carla's relief he didn't force the issue.

She heard the sound of him padding away from the door which told her he was in his bare feet and then the squeak of the old-fashioned bedsprings, which unfortunately didn't disclose any further information about his current state of dress.

Oh, grow up! she berated herself, counted to ten, then took a deep breath and pulled open the door.

The sight which greeted her on the other side, didn't diminish her anxieties in the least and Carla came to a dead halt. Clay was lying on his side, his naked torso reclining against the over-stuffed pillows, the lower half of his body covered only by a soft white sheet. His head was propped up on his elbow and his dark eyes were on her as she stood framed in the doorway. The skin of his bare arms and chest gleamed golden in the light from the brass lamp on the bedside table, but the glow in his eyes had nothing to do with the room's antique light fixtures. He looked like an indolent Middle Eastern sultan waiting for a harem girl.

Carla couldn't seem to move, though her legs were beginning to tremble so badly she feared if she didn't start walking she might not make it to the bed. Clay was looking at her as no man had ever looked at her before, seeing something in her that other men either didn't see or didn't notice. Even a virgin couldn't mistake the message in his eyes: Clay Chancelor found her very beautiful and desirable. He sensed the passion in her and he wanted that passion for himself. He wanted to make love to her.

In a split second, Carla accepted the fact that she wanted that too. She wanted Clay to be her first lover, had wanted it since the moment she'd first seen him.

Viewing the hunger in his eyes as he gazed at her body and feeling her response to that look, she couldn't deny the truth any longer. More than anything else in her life, she wanted to feel the full extent of this man's desire.

Without any doubt, Carla knew that Clay was the man she'd been searching for all her life, the man who would teach her about passion and provide the incredible pleasure that had always been missing in her other relationships. At long last, she was going to experience the shattering fulfillment that had only been possible in her dreams. Tonight was the night when all those romantic dreams would come true.

"Come to bed, Carla," Clay murmured hoarsely and she found herself moving toward him, as obediently as any harem concubine.

Barely able to draw breath, Clay watched her approach. She walked slowly, almost tentatively, but she knew exactly what her seductive pace was doing to him and she did it better than any woman he'd ever seen. Each movement of her slender body inflamed his senses until he felt on the verge of exploding.

Her magnificent breasts swayed with each step she took, her nipples hardening as they brushed against the delicate silk of her teddy. Her hair was even longer than he'd imagined it would be and even more beautiful. It tumbled down over her naked shoulders like a tawny curtain, the shimmering fall enriched by gleaming strands of russet and amber and bronze.

Her waist was so small that Clay was sure he could span it with his hands. Her hips were slender and her legs were long—long and lithe and lovely. He couldn't wait to feel them closing around his hips as he surged between them. He couldn't wait to feel her closing around him, all that sensuous beauty and feminine fire drawing him to her.

Clay had fantasized about making love to this woman many times since they'd met, but now that the time was actually upon him, he had to admit that all his dreams of how she would look naked had fallen far short of the mark. Nothing could have prepared him for this.

He'd known that she possessed a curvaceous figure beneath her businesslike clothes, but curvaceous didn't begin to describe this spectacular vision coming toward him. Considering the number of previous lovers that she'd had, Clay had taken a vow that he wouldn't suffer by comparison. Before she'd stepped out of the bathroom, wearing nothing but a provocative scrap of pink silk, he'd been determined to prove himself. He would be the man who gave her more pleasure than any of her previous lovers, the man who would take her somewhere unique and make her feel things she'd never felt.

Unfortunately, he couldn't seem to pull his feverish gaze away from her beautiful body or mask his expression, even knowing what kind of assumptions she was probably drawing from the sappy look on his face. Like an untried adolescent, he was practically drooling, and he had yet to touch her. Just the thought of it brought him close to losing control.

That realization inspired a fear that Clay hadn't experienced with any woman since his first. He closed his eyes to shut out the humiliating image, but the fear didn't go away just because he could no longer see Carla. He could feel the movement of the sheet as she lifted it, the dip of the mattress as she slipped into bed next to him, and the warm caress of her breath on his bare arm. He could feel her womanly heat and her scent surrounded him like the cotton sheets on the bed, smooth and warm and erotic.

With an abrupt motion that drew a startled gasp from the woman beside him, Clay rolled away from her and switched off the light. "We'd better get some sleep," he bit out tersely, praying that she didn't sense his problem and laugh at his last minute change of heart.

Until Clay had plunged the room into darkness, Carla had lain beside him without moving, her body as tense as a bowstring as she waited for his first touch. Now that she knew he wasn't planning to touch her, she willed her muscles to go limp, but she was far too keyed up to relax. Every nerve inside her was screaming for the feel of his hands, every inch of her skin was crying out to be stroked, every breath she drew was choked with frustration.

Why? Why had Clay looked at her as if he wanted to devour her, then turned his back on her as soon as she'd come within reach? And he'd sounded so angry. She couldn't understand his sudden rejection, nor his anger, and she would never get to sleep if she didn't find out what had gone wrong.

As suddenly as he'd lost his desire, she lost all of her pride. She needed to know what had happened, no matter how badly she might feel upon hearing his answer. "Clay? Did I do something to offend you?"

His muffled response was spoken into his pillow. "Don't be stupid."

Carla mulled that directive over in her mind for a few moments, then renounced it as unacceptable. "I don't think it's stupid for me to want to know why we aren't going to make love when it was perfectly obvious to me that you wanted to just as much as I did until a few seconds ago."

Clay rolled over onto his stomach, clenching one corner of his pillow in his hand. "Maybe I don't appreciate knowing how perfectly obvious I am to you."

Carla frowned as she propped herself up on both elbows. The room was dark but her eyes had adjusted and though his face was buried in the pillows, she could see the increased tension in his neck and shoulders whenever she so much as moved. "I don't think I understand what you're trying to tell me."

Clay didn't know how much more of this goading he could take. She was getting her kicks out of this situation, but he would be damned if he would put up with her taunting much longer. If she wanted it, then by God she was going to get it, no matter how dissatisfied she might be with the end result. He made one last effort to dissuade her from the dangerous course she was on, temporarily forgetting how much she enjoyed taking risks. "I'm warning you, Carla. Keep this up and you'll regret it."

"Keep what up?" Carla sat up in bed, clutching the sheet to her breast as she stared down at the rigid muscles of his back. She was becoming more confused by the second. She was also beginning to feel just a little angry. "You're the one who seems to have a problem."

"That does it," Clay growled, rearing up from the mattress like an enraged stallion. "If you like it hard and fast, you've got it."

One instant Carla was leaning back against the headboard and the next, she was dragged beneath six feet of powerful male muscle. She felt every inch of that textured length as Clay pinned her down with the weight of his body. Within seconds, her head was on the pillow, her hips and legs on an equal plane with his. She was aware of his nakedness with every breath she drew, aware of a searing heat that burned through her silk teddy as if it weren't even there.

Stunned by this unexpected assault and overwhelmed by sensations, Carla stared up into a pair of eyes that glittered like onyx and burned like coal. "Does it please you to know that I want you until I'm shaking with it?" Clay inquired bitterly, using all his strength to keep a grasp on the last measure of his control. "Does that kind of power excite you? I hope so, Carla, because I can't promise that I'll be able to wait until you're as ready to have me inside you as I am to be there."

He gave her a sample of his need as he moved his hips over hers, groaning at the ache in his aroused flesh as he brushed over the tender skin of her thighs. "If proof of my wanting makes me less in your eyes, so be it. Your triumph will only be temporary," he muttered thickly. "We'll just see how long you hold out the second time and the third and the fourth. Because I'm not stopping until you go crazy the instant

I touch you. I'm going to teach you a lesson some man should have taught you long ago."

Carla tried to speak but couldn't. She was too frightened by the images conjured up by his warning and then it was too late to say a word. He brought his mouth down on hers and her lips parted with a gasp. Instantly, he slid his tongue inside her mouth, thrusting deeply, setting a motion that would soon be matched by another part of his body.

Clay moved away only long enough to strip off her teddy then swept her beneath him again. Carla wasn't prepared for the heat that burned through her, nor the leashed force she could feel in the masculine body bearing down on hers. Terrified that he was about to release that driving power she arched up beneath him with an instinctive need to escape the unknown before escape became impossible. She knew she couldn't handle such a potent onslaught of passion her first time and whimpered with the knowledge that she didn't have any weapons strong enough to fight it.

Clay could feel the soft sounds she was making as the vibrations tickled against the back of his throat, but he didn't realize that they weren't the sounds of a woman's pleasure until he felt a shudder pass through her body and a cold clammy sweat of fear moisten her skin. For a few seconds, he couldn't believe what he was feeling. A woman who'd had such a variety of lovers as she'd had, couldn't possibly be afraid.

He lifted his mouth away to make sure he was imagining things and saw that he was not. Her blue eyes were wild with fear, her face ashen. Her breath came in ragged jerks through quivering lips. The truth

. . . be tempted!

See inside for special
4 FREE BOOKS offer

 Silhouette Desire™

Discover deliciously different romance with 4 Free Novels from

Silhouette Desire™

Sit back and enjoy four exciting romances—yours **FREE** from Silhouette Books! But wait . . . there's *even more* to this great offer! You'll also get . . .

A COMPACT MANICURE SET—ABSOLUTELY FREE! You'll love your beautiful manicure set—an elegant and useful accessory to carry in your handbag. Its rich burgundy case is a perfect expression of your style and good taste—and it's yours free with this offer!

PLUS A FREE MYSTERY GIFT— A surprise bonus that will delight you!

You can get all this just for trying Silhouette Desire!

MONEY-SAVING HOME DELIVERY!

Once you receive your 4 FREE books and gifts, you'll be able to preview more great romance reading in the convenience of your own home at less than retail prices. Every month we'll deliver 6 brand-new Silhouette Desire novels right to your door months before they appear in stores. If you decide to keep them, they'll be yours for only $2.24 each! That's 26¢ less per book than what you pay in stores—with no additional charges for home delivery!

SPECIAL EXTRAS—FREE!

You'll also get our monthly newsletter, packed with news of your favorite authors and upcoming books—FREE! And as a valued reader, we'll be sending you additional free gifts from time to time—as a token of our appreciation.

BE TEMPTED! COMPLETE, DETACH AND MAIL YOUR POSTPAID ORDER CARD TODAY AND RECEIVE 4 FREE BOOKS, A MANICURE SET AND A MYSTERY GIFT—PLUS LOTS MORE!

A FREE
Manicure Set
and Mystery Gift *await you, too!*

Silhouette Desire ™

Silhouette Books
901 Fuhrmann Blvd., P.O. Box 9013, Buffalo, NY 14240-9963

☐ **YES!** Please rush me my four Silhouette Desire novels with my FREE
Manicure Set and Mystery Gift, as explained on the opposite page.
I understand that I am under no obligation to purchase any books.
The free books and gifts remain mine to keep.

225 CIY JAX8

NAME _____
(please print)

ADDRESS _____ APT. _____

CITY _____ STATE _____ ZIP _____

Offer limited to one per household and not valid for present subscribers.
Prices subject to change.

SILHOUETTE "NO-RISK" GUARANTEE

- There's no obligation to buy—and the free books and gifts remain yours to keep.
- You pay the lowest price possible and receive books before they appear in stores.
- You may end your subscription anytime—just write and let us know.

If offer card is missing, write to: Silhouette Books, 901 Fuhrmann Blvd., P.O. Box 9013, Buffalo, NY 14240-9013.

hit him like a jolt of electricity and every muscle in his body convulsed in an agonized spasm. Earlier tonight, when he'd asked her if she'd ever been brutally assaulted, she'd lied to him! Some man had obviously hurt her, and hurt her badly.

Clay commanded himself to move off her, but the only part of him that could break through the feverish lust in control of his body was his voice. "Damn you, Carla. Why didn't you tell me?"

She answered him with tears, silent, miserable tears that rolled down her white cheeks and splashed onto his fingers like burning acid. Clay flinched with pain as the first drop hit his hand and swore with the next one. "God, I never wanted to hurt you. I thought you wanted it this way, that it excited you to have this kind of power over a man. The way you kept pushing at me, I was sure of it."

Carla swallowed painfully, taken aback by the self-disgust she saw in his eyes. "It's not your fault I'm a virgin," she whispered, averting her face as she felt the blood rush up beneath her skin. "I . . . I wasn't pushing for anything. I was only trying to understand what I did to make you not want me anymore."

Clay's breath hissed out in a savage burst. "A virgin!" He levered himself off her in one motion, flipped over onto his back and landed with a thump on the mattress. He heard her humiliated cry, felt her tugging frantically at the sheet that was pinned beneath his body, but the impact of her statement made it impossible for him to assist in her efforts to cover herself. Feeling the desperation in those efforts confirmed that she was telling him the truth, which meant that he had to rethink every thought he'd ever had about her. That realization was mind-boggling.

"A virgin," he repeated harshly, practically choking on the word. He lifted both hands to his head and raked his fingers through his hair. "Sweet heaven! The woman's a virgin...!" His voice trailed away as he tried to get a grasp on this unforeseen development.

Carla listened to the dark mutterings of the man lying beside her for several seconds before her embarrassment was replaced by the first inklings of temper. The throbbing blush that seemed to cover her whole body receded, then washed back in a different, much more vibrant color. Knowing Clay had a tendency to swear when he was confronted by something he didn't know how to handle didn't assuage her resentment one bit, and she didn't like hearing him speak of her innocence as if it were some communicable form of a dread disease.

She was just about ready to pull his arms away from his face and tell him what he could do with some of the more expressive words in his vocabulary, but as she reached for him, her gaze swept down the length of him and her hand stopped in midair. His body was sprawled out before her, a glorious feast for feminine eyes and she found that she couldn't do anything until she'd taken her fill of the sight.

It shouldn't have surprised her to see that the lower half of his body was just as beautiful as the upper, but somehow it did. His overwhelming maleness made her skin tingle just by looking at him. His legs were long, the clearly defined muscles of his thighs denoting a steely strength. Carla's stomach fluttered as she absorbed the broad shoulders and powerful chest, the narrow waist and hips, the flat abdomen that she knew felt hard and unyielding against her softness.

Whorls of black hair formed a wedge on his chest and tapered down to trail across his belly before widening at the apex of his thighs. She felt all shaky inside as she gazed at the part of him that would have joined with her if he hadn't sensed her fear and pulled back. She could almost feel what that moment would have been like, feel the strength and the uncompromisingly male rhythm he had already demonstrated to her with his tongue, and she ached for that moment again.

The tiny moan she emitted came with the memory of his tongue thrusting inside her soft mouth. She wanted to feel that again, too. For a few seconds, she thought she was imagining things, but then her eyes went very wide as the magnificence before her thickened and swelled in response to her vivid thoughts.

Her eyes flew to Clay's face. He was watching her watching him, reading her mind as if her need for him was written in huge block letters across her blushing face. "Keep looking at me like that, big eyes, and you'll find yourself with more trouble than you can handle."

Carla heard the warning, but refused to heed it. Part of his statement might be true but she could deal with anything he cared to dish out. Forgetting how poorly she'd dealt with his brand of passion just moments before, she lifted her chin in defiance. "I can handle anything."

"Oh?" Clay inquired, the sparkle in his dark eyes making her wish she had something to throw at him.

"Yes," she snapped forcibly, unaware that by rationing out enough sheet to cover him from waist to thigh, her actions belied her next words. "I'm not afraid of sex, I just haven't ever chosen to do anything."

"Might I ask why you've put off making that choice for so long?" Clay queried as he sat up and switched on the light. He seemed not to notice that the movement reexposed the parts of his body she most wanted covered. "You are getting up there, you know."

Carla bristled at his reference to her advanced age. "So what if I've waited? A woman's age shouldn't have any bearing on her decision to sleep with a man. It's her feelings that count. She should wait until it feels right, no matter how long that takes."

She didn't realize how much she'd revealed by that statement until Clay asked for further clarification. At the same time, he shifted his leg until it was touching hers, anticipating her physical response almost as much as her verbal answer. "And it felt right with me?"

Carla kept her eyes firmly fixed on his face, determined not to show her reaction to the feel of his naked thigh pressed against hers, but then he picked up a length of her hair and combed the shimmering length through his fingers. The intimate gesture constricted her lungs and it was all she could do just to breathe. And he knew it, damn him, he knew exactly what he was doing to her and was taking great pleasure in doing it.

Carla decided that the only way she could possibly disarm him, before she became the target for an entire arsenal of sensual weapons he had yet to deploy, was to take evasive action. "Yes. You met my qualifications."

"What qualifications?" Clay trailed one languorous finger down the bare skin of her arm and smiled as she shivered in response. He was rapidly learning that virgins weren't that much different from experienced women. All they required was a much slower pace.

"I wanted my first lover to be beautiful."

Clay blinked in surprise and his hand fell away from her hair. "Beautiful?"

Carla nodded gravely. "Of course, up until a few moments ago, I didn't know you were all-over pretty, but judging by your face, I felt certain you had to be and you are."

"All-over pretty," he mumbled incredulously, oddly embarrassed by the assessment. Pretty implied a dainty or delicate quality that he didn't particularly want applied to him. "What the hell kind of thing is that to say to a man? Men are handsome, not pretty."

It was Carla's turn to smile, but she didn't dare chance it. "With your long curly eyelashes, silky hair and classical features, you're beautiful. The first time I saw you, I thought you were obnoxious but perfectly lovely."

"Cut it out, Carla," he warned tersely, feeling his face starting to get hot.

If Carla had paid closer attention to the danger signs, she would not have stepped over the line that sealed her fate in Clay's mind, but she was too pleased with her tactics to retreat when she felt she had him on the run. "It isn't fair that a man should get such long eyelashes, that faultlessly smooth skin and beautiful waves in his hair. I bet your mother broke down in tears the day you had your first haircut."

If Clay didn't know better, he would have assumed that Carla had heard the sentimental story Georgine Chancelor told about that very event as often as she could to anyone who would listen. If he didn't know better, he would think that she'd been privy to all the embarrassing phrases his mother used to describe him as a child. Such a pretty boy, lovely as an angel, an utterly beautiful baby—he'd heard those descriptions from his mother too many times to count, but not since puberty had another woman described him in those terms.

Of course, none of the other women he knew had Carla's knack for pushing all the right buttons on him. Too bad for her that he'd recognized her expertise in that area on the drive to Connecticut and had re-solved not to overreact in the future. What she hadn't recognized yet, but was about to find out, was that he had the same talent where she was concerned and she'd recently exposed herself where she was most vulnerable.

"I know something else that isn't fair," he ac-knowledged, making sure that his voice held no hint of his inner amusement.

"What's that?" Carla queried.

"That you've seen enough of me to judge that I'm all-over pretty but I haven't taken advantage of the same opportunity. To maintain the status quo in our relationship, don't you think that I should?''

"I most certainly do not!"

"That's okay, pretty lady," Clay drawled silkily, as he began pulling on the sheet. "You soon will."

Seven

Carla refused to engage in a tug-of-war that she couldn't hope to win. Since Clay had more strength in one muscular arm than she had in her entire body, her only chance to come out of this situation with any part of her dignity intact was to retreat back into the relative safety of the bathroom. With that goal in mind, she let go of the sheet, hoping to catch Clay off balance as she made her escape.

Unfortunately, Clay was ready for that move and she wound up in the same position that she'd found herself in earlier, flat on her back beneath a naked male and staring up into a pair of sparkling hazel eyes. The sensation of Clay's body pressed against hers was just as shocking to her this time as it had been the last. "Let me go," she ordered curtly, praying he couldn't tell how close she was to panic.

"Now why would you want to leave me?" Clay asked curiously, as he gently pushed back the strands of hair that had fallen over her face. "I still meet your qualifications for a lover, don't I?"

"Very funny," Carla replied through tight lips, closing her eyes so she wouldn't have to see the triumph in his, but they immediately flew back open at his next words.

"And you meet all of my qualifications, too. Even without looking I can tell that you're far more lovely than I am, far more beautiful," he murmured, tracing the trembling bow of her lips with his thumb, then touching the corner of her mouth with his lips.

"I am?" Carla couldn't stop herself from asking, any more than she could prevent the tiny moan that escaped her lips when he kissed her so sweetly again. If this man kept on insisting that she was beautiful, kissing her as if she were exquisite, she just might start believing him.

"You are," Clay confirmed, laughing softly at her gasp when he tugged gently on the sensitive flesh of her earlobe. "But that's not why I want to make love to you so badly."

"It's...not?" Carla stammered, shivering helplessly as she felt the strong, hard length of Clay's body tenderly caressing the entire length of hers.

"No, it's not," Clay admitted. "The way you look isn't nearly as important as the way you make me feel. I've never reacted this strongly to any woman before. Whenever I get near you, it happens."

"What happens?"

Clay moved his hips slowly over hers, giving her physical proof of how much he wanted her. "This happens."

"Oh," Carla breathed, as a starburst of sensation exploded inside her.

Clay felt her instinctive response to the feel of his arousal and he stifled a groan. This had been their problem all along, he realized with sudden clarity. Every action he took brought an equal reaction in her whether they were laughing or arguing or making love. Whatever they tried to do, they were an equal match and that realization excited him beyond belief.

Carla didn't have enough experience to know what her volatile reactions to him meant, but by morning she would understand. He was going to show her the most thrilling kind of excitement any woman could feel. To ensure her enjoyment, however, he would have to admit his own vulnerability and let her know that his previous sexual experience didn't prepare him for this any more than she was prepared.

For her to attain the same sense of satisfaction that he desired for himself, they would have to enter into this situation just as they'd entered into every other encounter, on equal terms. "Before tonight, I had told myself that you were an expert at enticing men to the point where they couldn't think about anything but losing themselves inside you. Now I know otherwise, but I still need you so badly that I'm prepared to beg. So what do I tell myself now?"

Carla didn't know if Clay had an answer for that thought-provoking question, for even as he asked it he claimed her mouth in a kiss that tried to absorb her into himself. He had spoken of his need and she could feel that desire in his kiss, feel it and glory in it. This gorgeous man wanted her just as much as she wanted him and her inexperience made absolutely no difference to him. Hot, deep, slow...he caressed every honeyed curve of her mouth, pleading with his tongue for her to give him the same pleasure.

Carla couldn't deny him something that she wanted so much for herself, so she followed him, met him, and eventually astonished them both by surpassing him. She could feel Clay's surprise and his pleasure as she sought to taste more of him and that response inspired her to an even greater daring. She ran her fingertips over his lips, traced their outline with her tongue, then nuzzled his jaw and began stringing kisses down the side of his strong neck.

As Clay had feared, once Carla got over her initial inhibitions, it would take everything in him to keep to a pace that wouldn't frighten her off. She didn't know what her moist little kisses were doing to him. She would probably stop kissing him if she did, and he would rather die than have her stop. Yet, if he was going to last long enough to see to her pleasure, he had to get out of his current position. With his hips cradled between the silken warmth of her thighs, the need to thrust forward was almost unbearable.

When he felt her soft mouth on his chest, he could have ended his torment right there, but somehow he found the strength to hold back. "I like that too much," he murmured thickly, as he slid off her. "And so will you."

To Carla, his words didn't sound so much like a challenge as they did a loving promise, so she didn't resist when he grasped her shoulder to prevent her from turning toward him. She felt a bit threatened when he pinned her legs beneath the weight of his thigh, but then he lowered his head to her breasts and she felt nothing but pleasure. She gasped at the first skillful stroke of his tongue and she clutched the sheet as he drew her taut nipple into his mouth.

Carla's breath came faster and faster as Clay caressed her sensitive flesh with tongue and teeth. She cried out when he suckled, wholly lost to the sensual lightning that jolted through her body and centered itself in a blaze of heat between her thighs. When he brought his hand up to stroke her other breast, kneading it and rolling the tight peak between his fingertips, she didn't think she could stand it.

"Too...much," she agreed with his assessment of this kind of pleasure, only to hear him state that he had just begun. He swept his hand down from her breast to her thigh and a piercing fire ripped through her as he cupped the heat of her in his palm. Delicately, he teased the tiny, sensitive bud hidden in her softness and her body went wild.

Carla felt her hips echoing the rhythm of his fingers, but Clay was the one who shuddered with her movements as if he were in some kind of terrible pain. "Clay?" she queried urgently, concerned by the knotted rigidity of muscle she felt in his thigh as she squirmed beneath it, but unable to stop her response to his intimate caresses. She needed him, needed him to control the lightning that coursed through her, but when she reached for him, he pulled out of her arms.

"Oh, give me strength," Clay groaned as he moved away for a moment to ensure her protection. He was awed by what his slightest touch brought out in her. He closed his eyes for an instant, his face tormented by the sweet agony in his loins, an agony he had to endure even longer in order to awaken her fully. Then, as his touch slid more deeply into her, she threw her arms around his waist and pulled him down upon her writhing body.

"Make it stop," she pleaded, knowing that he possessed the driving power she needed to assuage the violent surges of feverish energy that were fast consuming her.

"Not yet," he moaned harshly, but she made it impossible for him to follow through with that denial. She gave a ragged little cry and arched against him, capturing him between her clenched thighs. He jerked reflexively, but instead of drawing away, his body surrendered to an instinct far stronger than any dictate of his brain. As much as he wanted to hold back until Carla was too far gone to realize what was happening, he was inside her and then it was too late. With one primal thrust, he broke through the fragile barrier and embedded himself in her soft heat.

"I...don't want to hurt you—" Clay's voice broke under the weight of his guilt, his whole body trembling with the effort to restrain himself until she had recovered from his possession. Sweat broke out on his body as he held himself still, sheathed in fire, yet unable to soothe the pleasurable agony. He could hardly believe it, when instead of pushing him away, she grasped hold of his hips, urging him forward again.

"More," Carla whispered in desperation, seeking the ecstasy that shimmered just beyond reach. She could feel the throbbing heat of him inside her and the searing pleasure of it more than made up for a split second of pain. The burgeoning warmth of him made her tremble and quake with a yearning that surpassed any fear she might have felt.

Clay lifted his head and stared straight into her eyes, stunned by the blind passion he saw in them. Bracing the lower half of his body on his arms, he tested the truth of what he saw and was instantly rewarded by the sight of her lips parting in a delighted gasp. "Are you sure, Carla?" he asked, still uncertain until he attempted to withdraw from her and she held him tightly in her arms.

Carla couldn't answer his concerned query with words, so she answered by giving more of herself. She opened to him, arching upward, taking all of him and telling him of her pleasure with each rapid breath. As Clay felt the tiny convulsions deep inside her, his control shattered.

Just before his strength gave way to a series of fierce explosions, he admitted to himself that this woman's greatest vulnerability was also her most potent weapon. He had claimed her innocence, but by her all-consuming passion, she had the power to possess his soul.

Carla clung to him as Clay moved faster and faster. The hot slick strokes that made her his were like nothing she'd ever dreamed of. At last, the escalating spiral of need burst inside her and she went up in flames, calling out his name as his body joined hers in the fire.

For long minutes they lay fused together, unmoving, as the ragged tempo of their breathing evened and slowed. Reluctantly, Carla became aware again, aware of herself and the man sprawled heavily across her. *Why on earth did I wait so long to feel this?* she asked herself in bemusement, appalled when she discovered that she'd spoken the words out loud.

With a low chuckle, Clay lifted his head away from her breasts. "Because it didn't feel right until you met me," he reminded her with blatant satisfaction. "And it wouldn't have felt this way with anyone else."

Carla didn't like his cocky tone nor the possessive gleam in his eyes as he gazed down at her kiss-swollen lips. She couldn't let him think that she belonged to him now, even if that was exactly how she felt. There wasn't any future in their relationship. As soon as they caught up with their grandparents, their brief affair would come to an abrupt end.

With that fact in mind, she asked skeptically, "How do I know it won't feel this way with just anyone?"

Clay's smile was indulgent as he very slowly, very deliberately withdrew from her and she couldn't prevent a tiny gasp of regret. As he shifted himself off to one side, the hair on his chest feathered over her nipples and they rose and tightened beneath his knowing gaze. "If that doesn't tell you, I guess you'll just have to take my word for it."

Furious with her body for revealing the exact nature of her feelings for this man, and furious with him for taking full advantage of that knowledge, Carla challenged recklessly, "I'd much rather find out for myself, thank you very much."

Clay's smile never wavered, even as he fought the jealous urge to tell her that if he had his way, she would never get the chance to find out what it was like to make love to any man besides him. It was much too early in their relationship for him to make such a declaration. She was having enough trouble dealing with what had already happened between them. And then, there was the pressing matter of their grandparents.

"We'll see," he offered with a nonchalant shrug.

"I'll see," Carla insisted stubbornly, blue eyes sparking for a fight.

Clay sighed and slid one arm beneath her, pulling her against him before she realized what he was doing. Ignoring her efforts to twist out of his grasp, he forced her head down upon his shoulder and threw his leg over her hips to keep her resisting body in place. "I know how you feel, sweetheart," he offered sympathetically as he pulled up the sheet to cover them both. "The first time is always the most overwhelming, but you're not alone in this situation. I didn't expect things to turn out this way either, and my emotions are just as raw as yours."

Patting her shoulder, he advised, "Just relax and try not to worry. This isn't the right time to sort things out. Save it until tomorrow when we've both had enough rest to be able to think straight."

Unbelievably, Carla felt her stiff muscles go slack, soothed by the warmth of his body, just as her mind was being soothed by his warm-hearted words. He refused to let her move and, within a few moments, she was overcome by an exhaustion that was just as unfamiliar to her as the stupefying emotions that had claimed her in the aftermath of a soul-burning passion.

"Tomorrow," she agreed, her lashes drifting down over her eyes as she gave up the struggle to stay awake.

The first thing Carla noticed when she opened her eyes once again was the bright sunshine streaming through the multi-paned windows. The next thing she realized was that someone was knocking on the door to their room. Lastly, she discovered that Clay Chancelor was an absolute bear in the morning, but she refused to dwell on the circumstances which made it possible for her to make that deduction.

"Dammit, woman! Knock off that racket," he growled into Carla's ear, seemingly unaware that since she was still lying beside him in bed, she couldn't possibly be responsible for the incessant series of loud raps that were coming from across the room.

"There's somebody at the door," Carla hissed, pushing at the heavy arm that was thrown across her waist and bucking her hips to dislodge an even heavier thigh. "One of us has to go see who it is."

Eventually, her squirming brought about the desired result but it didn't do a thing to appease Clay's bad temper. "Whoever's out there can come back at a decent hour!" he snarled in annoyance, rolled away from Carla onto his stomach and pulled the covers up over his head.

"Don't you dare go back to sleep!" Carla ordered firmly and Clay just as firmly ignored her.

"Just a minute please," she called out as she sat up in bed, searching for but not finding a clock. Even without one she could tell by the brightness of the room, that the person trying to awaken them hadn't arrived indecently early, but that they'd slept indecently late.

Judging by Clay's heavy breathing, Carla realized that it was up to her to answer the summons, but then she remembered that beneath the covers, she was stark naked. Several more seconds passed before she gave up the search for her teddy. The rest of her clothes were still hanging behind the door in the bathroom, which left her with no other choice than confronting the slumbering grouch once again.

"Clay Chancelor, if you don't get out of this bed right this minute and go answer that door, I'm going to give you a good swift kick," she warned him ferociously, enhancing the warning with a quick jab of her foot to the side of his leg.

"Okay, okay," Clay grumbled, struggling out from beneath the covers, and looking just as mean tempered as a black bear might look if he were being forced out of hibernation. Along with a night's growth of beard, his face wore a dark scowl. His hazel eyes were bleary and spikes of black hair were sticking up all over his head. Muttering under his breath, he got out of bed and stalked towards the door.

"Clay," Carla yelped before he pulled open the door. "You're not wearing any clothes."

"Huh?" Clay turned back to look at her, his expression vague until the fiery color of her cheeks burned through the cotton in his brain. He looked down at himself and back up at her blushing face, and suddenly became wide awake. Placing both hands on his hips, he demanded, "What the hell time is it anyway?"

"Don't stand there asking me stupid questions," Carla shrieked. "Put on your pants and see who's at the door."

"Better do what your old lady says, buddy." A gruff voice filtered through the wood. "I ain't got all day."

"Oh, lord." Carla pulled up her knees and dropped her burning face into her hands. "Frederick Valentine, I'll never forgive you for getting me into this!"

"That makes two of us," Clay said tersely as he pulled on his pants. With a brief glance over his shoulder to make certain that Carla was just as ready as he was to greet unwelcome callers, he pulled open the door.

"Okay, fella," he bit out as he surveyed a huge, barrel-chested man who looked as if he'd just crawled out of a grease pit. The man's face, hands, his tattered cap and patched coveralls were all coated with the stuff. "What's so urgent?"

"Hey, buddy! If you want to keep your woman in the rack all day, it don't matter to me, but if you want your wheels fixed, I'll have to see the color of your money," the man barked, in no better frame of mind than Clay.

Clay winced as he heard the gasp of outrage from the woman who still occupied the "rack" in question and swiftly concluded that he'd better get rid of their outspoken caller before he made a bad situation even worse. "You ever worked on a Porsche, Mister...?" he inquired, as he padded away from the door and went in search of his wallet.

"Sam Perkins," the man introduced himself, doffing his grease-spattered cap at Carla as he walked into the room. "Far as I know, one car's pretty much the same as any other."

"I'll take that as a no," Clay said dryly as he reached into the inside pocket of his suit-coat and removed his wallet.

Perkins assured, "Might take some time, but I'll figure it out once I get back to my garage. I got a manual on most every car ever made. Pay me twenty bucks for the tow and I'll get started on it first thing. Depending on the problem, I should have it back here by tomorrow."

"Tomorrow!" Clay and Carla exclaimed at the same time. Clay was about to elaborate on the unacceptability of that time frame when, to his amazement, Lucille Wiley scurried into the room, looking like a tiny bird who'd just had her feathers ruffled.

"I'm sorry for bursting in like this," she apologized as she crossed the floor and perched herself on the end of the bed. "But it was just the strangest thing, don't you know? Almost rude, if you know what I mean."

"What was?" Carla asked, peering over Lucille's shoulder to see if there was anyone else standing outside in the hall waiting to enjoy this impromptu morning get-together. Clay rolled his eyes, but Carla showed no surprise when William Wiley made his appearance in the doorway. She'd already resigned herself to the fact that some avenging angel had arranged this three-ring circus just so she would never be able to forget her first "morning after."

"Come in, Mr. Wiley," she invited, and even managed to smile.

"I'm very sorry for the intrusion," Wiley repeated his wife's apology as he stepped into the room. "But Lucy and I felt that you should know what just happened. I must say, I've never seen that kind of reaction in a couple who weren't under-age. As soon as we told them you'd arrived for the wedding, they got right back in their car and drove off."

"Damn!" Clay handed Perkins a twenty-dollar bill, then balanced himself on one foot as he pulled on a sock. "Did they give any indication where they were going?"

Lucille shook her head. "And it's such a lovely day for a wedding. I made my special punch and everything," she sighed, looking even more befuddled than usual. "I told them that too, but this new generation doesn't appreciate the personal touches like they used to when we were starting out. I don't know why I keep going out of my way for these people."

No one in the room pointed out that the people Lucille was berating were as far from being new generation as any two people could get. It just wasn't worth it. "We appreciate your efforts, Lucille," Carla felt obligated to say as she tried to come up with a polite way to get everyone to vacate the room so she could get dressed. Striving to appear casual in front of three relative strangers who had to realize that she was quite naked beneath the covers was becoming quite a strain. And Clay, the unfeeling jerk, seemed completely unconcerned about her plight as he engaged their guests in further conversation.

"How long ago did they leave?" he asked as he thrust his arms into his shirt.

"Not more than five minutes ago." Wiley gave Clay a considering look. "It was pretty plain that they didn't want the two of you to know where they were going. Do you have reason to be worried about them?"

"A very good reason," Carla confirmed, glancing down at her present position in the bed. "Though I'd rather not discuss it right now, if you don't mind."

"I don't mean to intrude on private family business," Wiley said, misinterpreting the message Carla was trying to convey. "Not knowing the problem, I probably shouldn't be telling you this, but your concern seems genuine."

"It is," Clay confirmed. "We're very worried about the state of my grandmother's health."

"In that case," Wiley said, "I did hear Mr. Valentine mention something about an airport."

"The only airport around is Statler's Field," Perkins put in helpfully.

"At least that's something to go on," Clay grumbled as he bent down to pick up his shoes.

"You're not leaving too?" Lucille asked reproachfully.

"Right away," Clay confirmed. "That is, if Mr. Perkins will give us a ride into town so we can arrange transportation to this airport."

"No problem," Perkins said, as he pocketed the second twenty-dollar bill Clay pressed into his palm. "Statler's Field is right on my way. What do you want me to do about your car?"

"Fix it," Clay ordered impatiently, directing a look at Carla that said, "get a move on, woman". She tossed back a glare that said she wasn't going anywhere until they got rid of their audience. Clay tilted his head toward the door. "You'll have to excuse us, but we're in kind of a hurry."

"Certainly." William Wiley got the message and walked over to offer his wife a hand up from the bed. "We'll make sure your bill is ready for you, young man."

"I'll get your car up on my rig," Perkins said as he walked out.

"All that punch," Lucille lamented as Wiley guided her toward the door. "I just can't figure people out, can you, Will, darling? They seem to get more inconsiderate every year."

Eight

Clay shifted his hips to find a more comfortable position and the woman tucked between his legs shivered. He couldn't tell if Carla was cold because of the wind that made his eyes smart whenever he peeked out from around her head to see the road, or if she was reacting to the feel of his body wrapped around hers like a sheltering blanket. Considering their current position in the back of a flat-bed truck, he didn't think it was a good time to inquire about the latter possibility.

Using his chin, Clay brushed her windswept hair to one side and spoke into her ear. "Are you freezing to death?"

Carla's voice caught on the wind, but Clay heard a surprising amount of exhilaration in her tone even if he couldn't quite make out her words. "I didn't hear that," he told her, hoping she didn't hear him groan as she twisted to face him and her soft bottom pushed up against his groin.

"It is chilly out here, but you want to know something strange?" Carla asked, gazing into his eyes, completely unaware of how stunning she looked with an animated expression on her face, blue eyes sparkling and her beautiful hair blowing free in the wind.

Clay didn't have to ask what was causing his shiver. "What?"

"I think I'm glad Sam didn't have room for us in the cab. Riding back here is kind of fun if you don't think about how easy it would be to fall off. I've never done anything like this before."

"Me neither," Clay admitted with a smile that took ten years off his face.

Carla returned his boyish grin, then swiveled around to continue her enjoyment of the sights. It was a beautiful spring day and they were traveling down a narrow, hilly road that was lined on each side by flowering trees and green shrubs. The smell of apple and cherry blossoms filled the morning air. It had been years since she'd taken the time to stop and smell the flowers. Today, with the sun on her face and the wind in her hair, she meant to do just that.

She no longer cared about the missing button on her blouse, the wrinkled condition of her black plaid skirt and the ever-widening run in her textured hose. Clay's elegant gray trousers were just as rumpled as her skirt and a long streak of grease marred the perfect crease on one pant leg. Her hair was a total mess and Clay was in definite need of a shave. Somewhere along the line, he'd lost his expensive silk tie and she'd lost an earring. Neither of them had anything to brag about when it came to their appearance, but this was an adventure and adventurers didn't worry about appearances.

Tilting her head back against Clay's shoulder, Carla said, "Freddie would love seeing me do something crazy like this."

"Why's that?"

"Because we have to be breaking several laws by sitting back here and to his way of thinking, I'm more law-abiding than is good for me."

Clay laughed. "Then we've got something in common. I've been told to loosen up more than once."

"By who?"

"Most often by my grandmother. She thinks I spend too much time at the bank." Clay felt Carla shiver again and any more thoughts about his favorite relative were pushed aside. "You are cold."

"Not really," she murmured vaguely, feeling the unsettling prickles she'd experienced a number of times since yesterday. So Clay's grandmother wanted him to loosen up a little, did she? Felt he worked too hard? Now wasn't that an intriguing coincidence?

Concerned for her comfort, Clay wedged his hips more securely between a three-foot-tall, metal tool chest and a wide steel beam that ran along the outside of the rig. He wished they could have ridden inside the Porsche, but that would have been even more dangerous. If that rusty looking winch let loose from the undercarriage of his car, it would go flying off the end of the ancient truck.

Tightening his arm around Carla's waist, Clay moved himself and her back several inches until his shoulders were leaning up against the wall of the cab where there was more shelter from the wind. "I must admit that hitching a ride on the back of a tow truck is a very novel experience, but I'm not sure if fun is the best way to describe it. Dangerous seems more appropriate, but then we both know how you feel about risks."

Carla couldn't have wished for a more effective gag order as a gust of wind swirled around the side of the cab and blew several strands of her hair into Clay's mouth. "For the tenth time, that aspect of my personality is as much a figment of your imagination as your belief that I was a man-eating femme fatale."

Clay's nose twitched as a delicate wisp of tawny hair tickled his nostrils. "This may surprise you, sweetheart, but I have yet to revise my opinion on that score. You might be inexperienced, but you're still one hot little tamale in bed."

"Well...really!" Carla sniffed, mortified by the picture he depicted, especially since it came so close to the truth. She swung her head around so he wouldn't see her telltale blush, unaware that the motion was as effective as a slap in the face.

Clay pulled the hair off his cheek, surprised at the sting. "Queen Victoria strikes again," he murmured indulgently, nuzzling his cold nose into the warmth at her nape. With his lips so close to her fragrant skin, he couldn't resist doing a little kissing. "Didn't anyone ever tell you that a woman who combines passion with innocence is the sexiest kind of woman there is?"

"If you don't cut that out," Carla warned, as a succession of delicious shivers ran down her spine, "I'm going to combine a sharp jab to the ribs with a swinging right hook."

"Well . . . really!" Clay mimicked and leaned away from her, smiling as her body unconsciously followed his movement, allowing no space between his chest and her back. He didn't particularly care whether she was motivated by a need for warmth or a liking for the feel of his body against her own. Whichever, he was thoroughly enjoying this situation.

To be truthful, he'd pretty much enjoyed every minute of the past eighteen hours or so. The circumstances that had thrown them together had not been exactly the best, but he couldn't recall when he'd had such a good time. His brows lifted slightly as he realized that he probably couldn't recall because for years he hadn't done much of anything that could even halfway be considered fun. As long as he could remember, his life had been one long series of exhausting business trips, complicated negotiations and boring meetings.

Even if he had taken the time to develop a romantic relationship with a woman, none of the females he knew would have agreed to ride in the back of a tow truck with him. This woman had not only agreed, she was actually enjoying herself. At least he hadn't been wrong in one respect pertaining to Carla. She was definitely one of a kind. "Hey!"

Sam Perkins took a curve too fast and Carla grabbed hold of Clay's thigh to keep her balance. Feeling her grasp so high up on his leg, Clay promptly lost his. They toppled over to one side, fell against the tool chest, then slid down its side as the truck swerved again. After that, they were subjected to several more lurches and bumps and Clay couldn't get a grasp on anything to pull them back up to a seated position. When they finally got through the rough section of road, Clay was lying on his back with Carla stretched out on top of him.

"Stop wiggling," Clay gasped as he felt the tight muscles of her derriere contract between his legs. "I'm on the bottom."

Carla's cheeks burned as she felt his response to her squirming. "So move already."

"We're wedged in here like a couple of sardines," he complained, but without much force. Nor did he show any inclination to right their positions.

Unaware of the beatific smile on his face, Carla concluded that he had to be stuck. Her hip dug into his groin as she tried to make additional room for them by pushing against the tool chest.

Clay grunted and took the hint. "Spoilsport."

With one arm wrapped firmly around her waist, he inched Carla and himself backward until he could reach the top handle of the chest. Before he pulled them up, he asked, "Are you sure you wouldn't rather stay down here all comfy and cozy? We could gaze up at that spring sky and admire all those puffy white clouds. Doesn't that sound like fun?"

"I've seen clouds," Carla told him primly, though she liked the sound of his suggestion far too much for her peace of mind. To be honest, she would probably enjoy doing anything with Clay. The more time she spent with him, the more time she wanted to spend with him. She hated to think about the moment when their escapade would be over and she would have to return to the mundane routine of her everyday life.

Once they were righted again, Clay queried at her ear, "Guess what?"

"What?"

In a slightly sheepish tone, he admitted, "I'm enjoying myself, too. Bankers aren't supposed to have fun you know. It's some kind of an unwritten law."

"Accountants aren't either," Carla replied, as she lifted her face to the warmth of the sun. "But I promise not to tell anyone about this, if you won't."

"You've got a deal." Clay gave her an affectionate hug and leaned back to enjoy the rest of their ride to Statler's Field.

Carla allowed herself to luxuriate in the feel of his arms around her for a few moments, then ordered herself to stop dreaming about something that could never happen. Clay Chancelor wasn't for her and never would be and she was kidding herself if she thought differently. For Clay, it was circumstances, not feelings, that had brought them together and those same circumstances would eventually force them to part.

Especially, if what she suspected turned out to be true. Clay would be livid and she had no doubt that she would be included in his anger. No matter how badly she would like to remain in his arms, she would be much better off if she told him of her suspicions now instead of later. At least that way, he wouldn't be able to accuse her of being in on the plan.

"Clay?"

"Hmmm?"

"Have you noticed that except for that kid at the gas station in Lockeford, we haven't seen anyone under the age of seventy since we got that phone call from George Byers?"

"Can't say I have," Clay replied, taking a deep breath to savor the smell of her hair.

"Well we haven't and I think that's odd."

"What's odd about it?"

"Every single person we've talked to has been around the same age as our grandparents. George, the rental agent, the Wileys, even Sam. I can't help but wonder if we're not part of some kind of conspiracy Freddie cooked up with a bunch of his old cronies to..."

"To what?" Clay felt her tense up and when she didn't answer, he grasped hold of her shoulders and turned her around to face him. To his amazement, he saw that she was blushing. "Carla, what kind of conspiracy are we talking about?"

She was already in for a penny and knew that Clay wouldn't let up on her until she was in for the entire pound. "Well, I'm not sure I'm right, you understand, but several strange things have happened since we learned of this elopement that make me think we were supposed to find out about it, drop everything and go chasing after them."

"What kind of things strike you as strange?"

Carla told him, starting with her reservations concerning the original phone call, which had come from a man who supposedly wanted nothing more to do with Freddie, to the rental agent whose granddaughter, just coincidentally, had run off to Wiley's Wedding Chapel. She ended with the feeling she'd had about the motto that hung above the chapel doors. "I can't tell you how many times Freddie's told me that I'd better start enjoying my life before it's too late, and I can't get over the feeling that he's finally decided to take matters into his own hands."

"I'm sorry, Carla," Clay apologized, "but that logic doesn't make much sense. Driving for hours in horrendous traffic, having our car break down, going without supper, then gobbling down a few doughnuts before bouncing around on the back of a tow truck doesn't strike me as the kind of enjoyable activities a loving relative would wish on a person."

"Believe me, when it comes to my grandfather, logic rarely applies," Carla informed him. "He probably took one look at my face the night I met you and decided to send us off together on this wild-goose chase."

"Why would he do that?"

Reluctantly, she conceded, "Because I couldn't hide the fact that I found you attractive and he thinks I need more romance in my life."

"He's got that right," Clay judged with a suggestive leer, refusing to take her concerns seriously. "And it's true that you find me an extremely handsome devil, though I wish you'd told me this earlier so I wouldn't have had to suffer through three weeks of frustration before my investigator came up with the perfect reason for me to find you again. You're a cruel woman, Carla Valentine."

Carla knew that he was teasing her about his motives for coming to her office yesterday, but his words delighted her all the same. "I apologize for the delay."

"And so you should," Clay admonished. "You have no idea how painful it was for me to accept that I was wildly attracted to a beautiful woman who had written me off as an arrogant snob with a small brain and a fat wallet."

Carla's mouth dropped open. "I could almost believe you really mean that!"

"Didn't I prove it to you last night?" Clay dropped a kiss on her open mouth. "No? Then I guess I'll just have to prove it again first chance I get."

Carla thought that was an excellent idea and reveled in the knowledge that he still wanted her. Then she remembered what they'd been talking about before they'd gotten off the subject, and she forced the pleasurable fantasy away. "If Freddie heard this conversation, he'd be springing cartwheels."

"You really believe that old man set this whole thing up?"

Carla sighed. "He's an incurable romantic."

"I see," Clay said thoughtfully, then agreed with her logic. "Yes, now that you've told me what the man is like, your deductions make perfect sense. Matchmaker that he is, your grandfather has kindly provided us with this incredibly romantic place to launch our affair. A chauffeured limousine might have offered us a bit more comfort, but being short on funds, Freddie must have decided to hire Sam Perkins and his trusty tow truck."

"You can laugh this off if you want to," Carla declared in exasperation. "But I'm not so sure that scenario isn't close to the truth. I'm telling you, Clay, I've been suspicious about this supposed elopement from the very first and nothing has happened to make me any less so. For instance, did you notice that we seemed to be the only guests at Wiley's? There were plenty of cars parked outside, but besides us, I never saw another living soul in the halls."

"If you and I were on our honeymoon, we wouldn't spend a lot of time walking the halls, either. I'd take you to bed and keep you there for days and days."

Carla sped past that conjecture, but she couldn't outrun the blush that mounted to her cheeks at the mere thought of spending days and days in bed with him. "What about food? No one could survive on Lucille's doughnuts for very long. I saw the kitchen, Clay, and it wasn't set up commercially. Other than the Wileys, I'd bet you anything that we were the only people there."

Clay could tell she was convinced of what she was saying. "I can see how life with your grandfather might tend to make one slightly paranoid, Carla, but you're forgetting something."

"What?"

"If your suspicions are true, my grandmother would have to be in on this plot," Clay reminded her. "Believe me, she's not the type to go along with such a half-baked scheme. She's a very straightforward lady. She makes no bones about the fact that she'd like to see me get married, and she does her share of matchmaking, but she'd never do something as devious as what you're suggesting. When grandmother wants to set me up with a woman, all she does is make an appointment for me to meet the lucky lady through my secretary.''

He chuckled at some memory. ''She knows I'd never break an appointment and she doesn't need to play a more complicated trick than that one. I've fallen for it every time.''

''Seeing as how you're still a bachelor, I wouldn't be so sure that she hasn't come up with a new approach,'' Carla suggested. ''I'm beginning to believe that our grandparents think an awful lot alike.''

''Which is probably why they decided to run off and get married,'' Clay concluded firmly. ''The reason my grandmother moved to Ridgeport is because she needed the company of people her own age. She'd been very lonely since my grandfather died.''

Carla gave up. ''Okay, have it your way, but don't say I didn't warn you.''

Three miles farther down the curving road, Perkins turned the truck off onto a graveled drive and pulled to a stop in front of a long, rickety wooden building. ''This is an airport?'' Carla cried, surveying the building and the surrounding grass field with incredulity.

''Sam?'' Clay inquired as the man came to help them down from the rig.

Perkins shrugged. ''It may not be La Guardia, but it's all we've got.'' He pointed to the dilapidated building. ''You'll find Harvey Statler inside behind the counter. He owns the place. I know it doesn't look like much, but Harv offers a complete charter service. He runs a real good business.''

''Business can't be too good. I don't see any cars or any planes,'' Clay said, staring up at the top of the hangar where what was once a directional gauge hung from a pole like a limp sock worn full of holes. ''Is there even a landing strip?''

''Sure,'' Perkins said. ''It's out in back, same as the parking lot. The pavement's not too good in the lot. I didn't want to risk your car falling off the rig if I hit a pothole. That's why I stopped out in front.''

''Let's walk around the building and see if their rental car is in the lot,'' Carla suggested. ''That will tell us if they're here.''

''In the off chance that they are, I'd rather nab them inside,'' Clay negated her suggestion. ''That way we can cut off the old man's escape route before he high-tails it again.''

Carla turned up her nose at his phrasing. ''I wish you would stop referring to my grandfather as if he were a felon on the run.''

''If he marries my grandmother before I catch up to him, that's exactly what he will be.''

Carla used a Freddie Valentine expression to state her opinion of Clay's threat. ''Poppycock! He hasn't broken any law.''

Clay opened his mouth to dispute that opinion but Sam Perkins cut him off. ''Look! You two can stand around arguing all day if you want to, but I've got a business to run so I'll be on my way.''

Clay didn't think it would be wise to let Perkins go. ''There'll be some extra money in it for you, Sam, if you wait here until we find out if we've come to the right place. We won't be long. My grandmother prefers to fly first class, so I doubt this is where they were heading."

"Okay by me," Perkins agreed and climbed back up in the cab.

Clay reached for Carla's hand and they began walking toward the building. "Unless I miss my guess, we're still going to need that ride into town."

"We can live in hope," Carla muttered feelingly under her breath.

Once inside the hangar, they walked past two antique propeller aircraft, entered a door marked office, then proceeded down a long hallway until they reached a formica counter. As Perkins had predicted, that's where they found the owner.

Harvey Statler was seated behind a wide metal desk, reading a copy of *Sports Illustrated*. The desk was cluttered by stacks of dated magazines, used paper cups, nuts, bolts and other sundry mechanical parts. Statler looked like an old World War II fighter pilot, in a brown leather, fur-lined flight jacket, leather hat with earflaps and a white woolen muffler. Though he was thin and muscular, he was well past retirement age.

"Another senior citizen," Carla whispered.

Clay pretended not to hear her. The man's age was irrelevant. After one look at the elderly flying ace and his shabby surroundings, Clay had known that their trip to Statler's Field had been a total waste of time. Lillian Chancelor would never arrange for a flight from this pitiful excuse of an airport or board one of those old relics they'd seen parked in the hangar.

"We may as well forget it," Clay said, grasping hold of Carla's elbow.

"Can I help you folks?" Statler lifted his head from his magazine before they turned away from the counter.

"I don't think so," Clay told him. "Sorry to bother you."

The man went back to reading his magazine. "No bother," he mumbled as Clay and Carla retraced their steps down the hall. They could hear him talking to himself as they walked away. "Sorry, Rosie, it looks like that old couple is all the business we're going to get today."

Within seconds they were back at the counter. Clay did the talking for them both. "Did you say something about an old couple?"

"Yup." Statler gazed over his shoulder at a clock. "Took off for the Catskills about twenty minutes ago."

Carla exclaimed. "The Catskills! Why on earth would they go there?"

Clay ignored Carla's outburst. "Could you tell us the names of these people?"

Statler cocked a suspicious blue eye up at Clay. "Could, but that ain't sayin' I will."

Carla issued a warning under her breath, "Freddie probably paid him to keep his mouth shut."

Clay shot her a silencing look. To Statler he said, "If the woman's name was Lillian Chancelor, she left the house this morning without her heart medication.

I've got to find out where she went so I can bring it to her. I'm her grandson and I'm very concerned for her health.''

"Medical matter, huh?" The chair creaked as Statler got up and came over to the counter. He shuffled through some papers until he found what he was looking for, then said, "Yup, that's the name on the flight plan."

"So much for your first-class theory, smart guy," Carla declared sweetly.

Clay shook his head, still finding it hard to believe that the elegant lady he'd known all of his life would have anything to do with this two-bit operation. "The man's name was Valentine? Correct?"

"Valentine, Frederick, destination The Laurel House." Statler read out loud. "With a good tail wind, they should land in about an hour. If you want to wait around 'til then, you can put in a call to them."

"You've heard of The Laurel House, haven't you, Clay?" Carla asked.

"No."

"It's a luxury hotel catering to the young and wealthy. A perfect setting to inspire a little romance, wouldn't you say?"

"Not ours," Clay insisted, though he wasn't quite so opposed to her theory as he'd been a short while earlier. "Our grandparents are young at heart and they both have very expensive tastes."

As soon as the words were out of his mouth, Clay frowned. Expensive taste was still another, in a growing list of personality traits, that the elderly couple appeared to hold in common. Was it possible that the two of them also agreed on the fact that their grand-children would be perfect for each other? Or were their grandparents perfect for each other because of the abundance of similarities in their personalities?

The only way to find out was to catch up with them. "Mr. Statler, we need to get to The Laurel House as soon as possible. Can we charter a plane and a pilot to fly us there?"

"Sure thing. Me and Rosie are always gassed up and ready to go," Statler boasted.

Clay didn't want to know who the "me" was in that statement, and he was even more reluctant to learn the identity of "Rosie." "You name your airplanes, Mr. Statler?"

"Nah," Statler said, pulling open a drawer in the counter and lifting out several sheets of paper. "Only her. We've been together so long that she's like a wife to me. I just have to fill out the paperwork and make the financial arrangements and we'll be ready to take off."

Carla prayed she wasn't hearing right when Clay said, "Fine" and knew that she had when he asked her, "Carla, do you want to go tell Sam he can leave now?"

She let out a long-suffering sigh. "No, but I will."

Nine

Carla was taken aback by Clay's delighted exclamation when they walked out the back door of the hangar and got their first glimpse of "Rosie." "What on earth are you grinning about? We'll be lucky if that old crate makes it off the ground."

To her surprise, Clay not only appeared to recognize the antiquated silver airplane parked on the narrow landing strip, he seemed thrilled by the prospect of flying in it. "That old crate happens to be a Gullwing Stinson," he told her, his dark eyes alight with appreciation. "No wonder Statler's so proud of her. She's a classic. The one I built was almost an exact replica of this one, right down to the *Marvel Mystery Oil* decals and the red lightning bolt on the fuselage."

"You built an airplane?"

Clay grabbed hold of her hand and pulled her reluctant form with him as he strode briskly across the tarmac. "Well, I was about six at the time, so my grandfather had to help me a little. Building model airplanes was a hobby of his and he got me started as soon as I could tell a rudder from an aileron. We must have built a hundred of them by the time he died. We even put together a Langley, the first heavier-than-air flying machine."

"Wow! Gee wiz, a Langley," Carla enthused dramatically, since she was obviously supposed to be impressed. Unfortunately, she wouldn't recognize an aileron if one jumped up and bit her and the only Langley she knew was her parents' butler.

Clay was in such high spirits, he didn't take offense at her facetious response to his boast. "Samuel Langley was a pioneer in design aviation. He failed in two trials to get a manned flight off the ground in 1903. If he'd succeeded, his name would be as recognizable today as Orville and Wilbur Wright's."

"Langley didn't have anything to do with the design of this plane, did he?" Carla inquired dubiously, as they approached the craft.

"Langley died in 1906. The Gullwing didn't come along until the 1930's," Clay apprised her knowledgeably, not noticing that she didn't take much comfort in the knowledge. "There's the step. Grab onto the strut and jump up, then swing yourself through the door."

Much against her will, Carla grabbed and jumped, but refused to swing. "Why do I have to go in there first?"

"Because my elders taught me that ladies are always seated before gentlemen."

"Just make yourself comfortable inside," Statler directed Carla as he walked up behind Clay. "As soon as I start the propeller, we can take off."

He handed Clay a wicker basket and two blankets. "Here's your lunch and some lap covers. Sometimes it gets a little chilly up there."

"Thanks." Clay reached up and gave Carla a pat on the leg, encouraging her to do as their pilot asked. When she didn't comply, he hopped up behind her and pried her fingers loose from the strut. "Come on, where's your sense of adventure? This is going to be fun."

Ten minutes later, her stomach lurching, Carla hollered so she could be heard over the loud roar of the engine and the whirring propeller. "Is this the fun part? Am I having fun now?"

"You're having a ball," Clay shouted back, gazing raptly out the window. "We're way above the trees."

"I'm so glad to hear that," Carla muttered sarcastically, though his words did give her the courage to open her eyes. The first thing she saw was Clay, pressing his nose against the window like a kid in front of a candy shop. He didn't even seem to notice that this particular window was vibrating like a marimba. "This part of our trip must have been Lillian's idea. Freddie knows I hate to fly."

Clay turned to look at her. "Did you say something?"

Knowing what Clay thought of her theories, Carla didn't repeat what she'd said. The man refused to believe that his grandmother had a devious bone in her body. "Are we there yet?" she yelled, trying to sound like a child who had no idea of distance, but was already bored with the ride.

Clay smiled and lifted the wicker basket onto his lap. "Why don't we eat our lunch. This will help pass the time."

"Okay," Carla agreed. "I'll have a Dramamine sandwich."

Noting her pallor, Clay was immediately all concern. "Are you going to be airsick?"

Carla almost said yes, but then realized that her stomach seemed to have settled down. "Maybe later," she shouted. "At the moment, I'm far more worried about going deaf."

Clay nodded. "It is pretty loud back here." Pointing to the cockpit, he shouted, "Being the pilot is better. Then you get to wear earphones."

"Do you fly?"

"I've got my license, though it's been a long time since I've done any flying." A nostalgic look came over his face. "My grandfather took me up when I was a little kid, then taught me to fly when I was still in my early teens. I didn't know that was his intention until one day he let go of the stick. He told me that the best pilots were the ones who could fly by the seat of their pants and advised me to get the feel of the plane quickly or we would hit a tree."

"What did you do?"

"It was an open cockpit." Clay chuckled in remembrance. "We had to pick a few leaves out of our hair, but I managed to keep up in the air."

Watching his face as he recounted the story, Carla couldn't help but wonder whether Clay's main reason for opposing his grandmother's remarriage was his fear of her getting hurt, or whether he was hurt by what he saw as her disloyalty to a man that he'd obviously loved very, very much. "Your grandfather sounds like quite a character."

"That he was," Clay agreed with a smile. "Most people knew him as a shrewd businessman with an almost uncanny grasp of the money market, but I got to see the easygoing side of his nature. He was just as happy building model airplanes as he was negotiating a new deal for the investment firm."

"How long ago did he die?"

Not long enough to erase the grief, Carla noticed, as Clay answered, sadness in his eyes. "He's been gone about eight years now."

Suddenly, a look of surprise replaced the sadness. "This is the first time I've been up in a small plane since his death. With him gone, it just wasn't as much fun for me anymore."

If it hadn't been so noisy, Carla would have liked to hear more about Clay's childhood and his relationship with his grandfather. As it was, they had to strain their vocal cords to talk and strain their ears to understand. By mutual agreement, they gave up trying and turned their attention to the food Harvey Statler had provided for them.

To Carla's amazement, she was able to finish off a large chicken sandwich, a small bag of potato chips and three brownies with no ill effects. But she wasn't allowed to enjoy the contented feeling very long. One minute she was relaxing back in her seat of stretched canvas and the next she was pressing herself against Clay, her hands clutching his arm.

"We're going to crash!" she screamed as the engine coughed and sputtered, then died.

Her scream was loud enough to get through to their pilot who immediately called over his shoulder, "Not to worry, miss. Old Rosie is just having one of her spells. She'll be right as rain again as soon as I do a little readjustment on her carburetor."

Carla wasn't the least bit reassured by this announcement until she looked over at Clay and saw that he wasn't any more worried than their pilot. "Why aren't you scared?" she demanded, unable to understand why she was the only one who appeared to be concerned by the loss of their engine and the rapidity of their descent.

"There's no reason to be frightened," Clay replied calmly, wincing slightly as he pried her clutching fingers off his arm. Keeping hold of her hand, he began stroking her sweaty palm. "Just relax, sweetheart. Rosie's a glider. We should be able to land even without an engine."

"Should!" Carla squeaked, once again on the verge of hysteria. "We *should* be able to? What if we can't?"

Statler shouted back over his seat. "No doubt about it, miss. We can land without any trouble at all. I'm setting Rosie down in that cornfield right over there and she'll circle in between these hills just as pretty as a seagull landing on the water."

"If you noticed, the wings are shaped like a gull's," Clay said, trying to enhance her belief in Statler's promise, even though he knew they were in real trouble. Glancing out the window, he could see the fortresslike ledges and steep gorges of the Catskill Mountains that their pilot dismissed as mere hills. "Harv will pick out an air current and we'll glide in as smoothly as a bird."

Not wanting to appear a coward, Carla subsided, though her fingers closed over Clay's hand like a vise. "If you say so."

For the next several minutes, the only conversation in the cabin was conducted by the pilot. Statler spoke to his elderly plane as if it were a recalcitrant female who needed to be cajoled into following his instructions.

"C'mon darlin', don't get yourself into a dither." Statler patted the dash, then eased back on the wheel. "I'll have you all fixed up in just a few minutes. All you have to do is hand over some gas so we can land."

Amazingly, the engine coughed and sputtered back to life the second Statler made his request. "That's my girl," the man complimented her affectionately. "Now let's ease on down, nice and gentle like the lady you are."

Carla gaped when the engine gave what sounded like an indignant little sniff, then resumed in a steady drone. She glanced over at Clay to see what he made of this conversation and was gratified by the incredulous look on his face. "No one would ever believe this," she declared firmly.

"That's for sure," Clay replied.

Carla was about to question him when Statler shouted, "Hold on folks. It might get a tad bumpy from here on in."

Carla didn't dare look out the windows. She closed her eyes and didn't open them again until she knew they were safely on the ground. She was so happy to be there, she didn't even challenge their pilot on his description of a "tad." Though they'd touched down then bounced back up into the air a number of times in the process of landing, she still had all her teeth and she hadn't lost her lunch, so what did she really have to complain about?

When Clay helped her down from the plane, she wanted to kiss the ground, especially when she saw how little of it there had been to permit a landing. Their precious cornfield was tucked in a narrow, tree-lined valley between towering summits that seemed to roll along the horizon like gigantic waves.

Clay must have read her mind. "Will I do instead?" he inquired with an understanding grin, then pulled her into his arms and planted a big kiss on her startled mouth.

"You're quite a woman, Carla Valentine," he murmured approvingly, and kissed her again.

Before they could become any more deeply embroiled in the passion that instantly flared between them, Statler walked around from the other side of the plane. Pointing across the field, he asked, "Mr. Chancelor, would you mind walking over to that house and seeing if they've got a few tools we can borrow? I need a box-end wrench and a screwdriver so I can inspect the fuel strainer."

"Not at all," Clay said, removing his hands from Carla's shoulders.

"Once I clear the lines, we can get right back up in the air. As the crow flies, we're less than forty minutes away from our destination," Statler reported. "With the tail wind we've got, we can make up this delay in no time."

"I'll go with you," Carla offered as Clay started walking.

"You're wearing heels," Clay reminded her, turning back to find her treading carefully over the uneven, furrowed ground. "Wouldn't you rather wait here? You can make yourself comfortable in the plane."

"Are you kidding?" Carla asked him, slipping off her shoes and stuffing them into the front pockets of her jacket. "The wild blue yonder is a bit too wild for me. I want to feel good old terra firma under my feet while I still can."

"They're your feet," Clay allowed, amazed that she would prefer walking across a stubbly cornfield in her stocking feet to a comfortable wait inside the plane. Most of the women he knew would have balked, but then he'd already accepted the fact that Carla wasn't like most women.

"Why don't you take those things off, too," he suggested, gesturing to her shredded hosiery. "They're a mess."

"Not a chance," Carla declared, surprising him with her vehemence.

Noting the lift of his eyebrows, Carla explained, "When we catch up with Freddie, I intend for him to see every bit of damage he's done to me with his latest scheme. With any luck at all, I'll cut my foot on something during this walk and develop a pathetic limp.''

Clay laughed and threw an arm around her shoulders. "Kid, you've been hanging around me too long. You're beginning to sound a little bloodthirsty.''

"I'm going to have his head on a platter," Carla began quoting her mentor. "I'm going to wring his neck. When I get my hands on him, I'm going to—''

"Atta girl," Clay complimented. "And he'll deserve it, but you don't deserve a limp. When we finally meet up with the old rascal, you can fake it if you want to, but you've been through enough without adding injury to insult.''

Turning his back on her, he bent down from the waist. "Hop on. We'll go piggyback.''

"I'm too heavy for you and my feet are all dirty," Carla protested. "I'll ruin your beautiful suit.''

Clay straightened to look at her, placing his hands on his hips. Tongue in cheek, he proposed, "How's this for vengeance? My suit is close to being in the same shape as your hose and if I develop a hernia from carrying around a featherweight like you, I can include my doctor's bill with my dry-cleaning charges and send them both to your grandfather. Then, for good measure, I'll hit him up for the cost of my tie. It was one of my favorites.''

"Good plan," Carla agreed, feeling too guilty over the damages he'd sustained to remind him that she paid all of her grandfather's bills.

Freddie being Freddie, he would not only skip out on the debt, he would probably present her with a bill for services rendered. Knowing how his mind worked, Carla was sure he would feel that she owed him a debt of gratitude for providing her with the chance to reel in one of the country's most eligible bachelors. From her grandfather's point of view, if she chose to cut bait before the well-heeled fish was securely captured in her net, it would be her fault, not his.

Once Carla was properly positioned on his back, Clay started to jog. The sooner they got this show back on the road, the sooner they would arrive at The Laurel House. No matter how much he'd enjoyed the last several hours, he was looking forward to taking a long, hot shower, changing out of his rumpled clothes, and eating a huge meal in a decent restaurant. He was also looking forward to making love to Carla again, though that might have to be postponed for a while, depending on what they found once they arrived at the hotel.

Carla was understandably upset with her grand-father, had even voiced a few threats, but time and time again, she'd shown him that blood was still thicker than water. She might malign her grandfa-ther's character, but woe to any other person who tried to do the same. Her loyalty to Freddie was unswerv-ing no matter what kind of trouble he got himself or his granddaughter into.

Clay realized that when he had told her his plan for exacting monetary vengeance on Freddie, the only reason she had let him go on was that she'd known he was teasing. Unfortunately, Clay knew his own temper. He would take one look at the old duffer and probably blow his stack. Carla would jump to her grandfather's defense and then the whole thing would escalate into a slanging match.

That kind of confrontation could easily destroy the wonderful relationship they'd started to build. And Clay wanted that relationship to continue, more than anything he'd wanted in a long, long time. No matter how enraged he felt whenever he thought about his grandmother being married to an unprincipled scoundrel, he couldn't lose control. To keep Carla, he was going to have to go easy on Freddie Valentine.

Even though it would mean a reevaluation of everything he believed about his grandmother, Clay was half beginning to hope that Carla's suspicions about Lillian's involvement in this would turn out to be true. That would mean she'd never intended to marry a man who wasn't Clay's grandfather, and Clay would much rather accept that than acknowledge Lillian's relationship with a man who couldn't possibly live up to the standards set by Barclay Northrop Chancelor I.

If Freddie and Lillian had stuck their heads together and concocted this outrageous scheme to bring their grandchildren together, Clay would still be angry, but nowhere near as angry as he would have been just a few days earlier. He didn't like being manipulated. But even without any further manipulations on anyone's part, deceitful or otherwise, Clay knew he was well on his way to falling in love with Carla.

At the edge of the field, Clay let Carla down and they started walking across a grassy lawn, toward the two-story, white clapboard house. "What if nobody's home?" Carla asked.

Clay shrugged. "I doubt anyone will mind if we borrow a couple of tools."

"Oh no," Carla said. "I draw the line at breaking and entering."

"But think how proud your grandfather would be of you if you could add robbery to your growing list of crimes?"

Carla swiftly rejected that argument. "Freddie is a thief of hearts, not a second-story man. He makes it easy for people to give him their money, but he'd never just out-and-out steal something. That would make him a common criminal."

Clay shook his head. "Amazing."

"Yes he is," Carla proclaimed proudly, and Clay thought better of bringing up the matter of Freddie's term in jail. The old man had probably convinced her that someone else had impersonated that French ambassador and forged his name on a series of bad checks from a phony bank account. Obviously, Freddie had been a victim of a gross miscarriage of justice.

They reached the house, mounted the front steps and entered the screened-in front porch. They both noticed the envelope tacked to the front door, but before either of them could reach for it, they heard the sound of an engine. "Sounds like we won't need those tools after all," Carla declared happily.

"What the hell!"

"What's wrong?" Carla cried as Clay grabbed her hand, pulled her down the porch steps, and started running toward the field. Then she saw what had prompted their mad dash. She saw it, but she stead-fastly refused to believe it, even as she watched their supposedly impaired plane lift off the ground and soar up into the air. "I know what he's doing. He's taking Rosie up for a test run. That must be it. He'll be right back as soon as he's certain the plane is safe."

"Wait here," Clay ordered in a tone that gave Carla little reason to expect that her assumption was cor-rect. The horrible feeling she had in the pit of her stomach was reflected on his face. Refusing to give up hope, she turned her eyes back to the sky as Clay ran toward the house.

He was back in less than two minutes, handing Carla the envelope that had been tacked up on the front door of the house. "Statler won't be back," he stated grimly, glaring up at the brilliant blue sky. "You've been right all along."

The object of that glare ascended to a level clear of the surrounding elevations, then disappeared behind a puffy white cloud. Inside the cockpit, Harvey Stat-ler adjusted the frequency on his radio. "Statler call-ing Chapel. Do you read, Chapel?"

A breathy female voice came back. "Hi Harv. Sam and Will are out returning cars and Lillian and Fred-die went up for a nap. We didn't expect your call to come in so soon."

"Picked up a tail wind."

"What should I tell them, Harv?"

"Tell them to break out the champagne, Lucy girl," Statler announced gleefully. "Mission accom-plished."

Ten

We're stranded here for four days!" Carla exclaimed angrily, crushing Freddie's note in her hand as she and Clay stomped up the stairs to the front porch. "What are we supposed to do with ourselves for four long days!"

"Guess," Clay suggested pointedly.

"Surely you don't think they expect us to...to—"

"Of course, they do, since I'm sure they've been told that we already have."

"Oh!" Carla cried, horrified by the realization that what Clay said was probably true. For all they knew, Freddie and Lillian could have been staying at the Wileys the whole time they were there. Even if their grandparents hadn't been there, Carla was sure that their fellow conspirators had taken great delight in reporting what they had seen in the bedroom this morning. It had been perfectly obvious to everyone how she and Clay had spent the night together.

As the written instructions contained in Freddie's note specified, Clay lifted up the welcome mat. "And here we have the key to our romantic bungalow."

"This situation is...this has to be the..." Carla couldn't find the right words to describe the kind of situation this was. "I've never been so angry in my whole entire life!"

"They've pulled quite a number on us," Clay admitted, though his tone didn't convey anger as much as it did self-mockery. "Until I came up against the Valentines, I never thought of myself as a gullible person."

"Don't include me in that condemnation," Carla said tartly. "After today, I'm severing all relations with my grandfather. I've put up with a lot of his she-nanigans in the last two years, but this time he's really gone too far."

"At the moment, I'm not viewing my grandmother any too fondly either," Clay acknowledged, finally accepting his own relative's culpability. "She knew how hurt I was by this supposed engagement of hers and took advantage of it. Until I saw that plane taking off, I never would've believed she was capable of conspiring against me like this."

"According to the note, she and Freddie have been good friends for years," Carla sighed. "Where on earth do you suppose they could have met?"

"I have no idea, but it's one of the first things I intend to ask her," Clay affirmed, as he bent down to insert the key into the lock. Pushing open the door, he waited for Carla to precede him, then followed her across the threshold. Silence reigned for several moments as they surveyed their new surroundings.

The front door had opened onto a large room that was partitioned off into three sections, one for eating, one for sleeping and one for sitting. Blue plaid curtains hung on all the windows and were tied back so they would not obscure the light or conceal the marvelous view of the mountains.

The kitchen area was off to the right of the door and consisted of a small trestle table with two chairs, an L-shaped oak counter and a wide buffet with open shelves that displayed a colorful collection of pottery. At the back of the room was a canopied daybed, enclosed by a cascade of the same bright plaid fabric as the curtains. Next to the daybed was a tall, narrow chest with seven drawers and a small table covered with magazines. An antique writing desk was tucked under a nearby window and a mammoth bookcase filled the remaining space on the rear wall.

The other half of the room was all living space, centered around a red-brick fireplace. Facing the fireplace was a long blue over-stuffed couch lined with bright floral cushions and a comfortable looking brown leather recliner. Picturing himself seated in that chair with his feet up, holding a snifter of brandy in one hand as he gazed into a warm cheerful fire, Clay enthused, "They couldn't have found a nicer place."

Under other circumstances, Carla might have agreed with him, but she was in no mood to discuss the comfort of their accommodations. "For a prison you mean."

Clay laughed at the outraged look on her face. "If you take that attitude, how are we going to have a good time?"

"We're not," Carla insisted darkly, as she followed Clay into the room. "I refuse to give them that satisfaction."

Clay nodded, striving to maintain a serious expression in the face of her heartfelt indignation. He doubted that she would appreciate hearing how beautiful she was when she was angry. Her eyes were brilliant and her color was high, reminding him of how she'd looked last night when her passion for him had been at its peak. He didn't think it was a good time to remind her of that now.

"I agree," he stated obligingly. "It would serve them right if we're miserable the entire time we are here."

Carla couldn't help but notice that Clay didn't look very miserable as he took off his suitcoat and tossed it down on the floral seat covering of a nearby ladder-back chair. When he kicked off his shoes and walked across the pegged hardwood floor to check out the fireplace, she got the feeling that he intended to make himself right at home. "Nice of them to supply us with firewood," he commented. "It probably gets cold here at night."

"What difference does that make since we won't be building any fires?"

Clay turned back to her, his head cocked at a questioning angle. "Why not? As long as we're stuck here, I don't see any harm in making ourselves comfortable."

"That's it? You're giving up just like that?" Carla threw up her hands incredulously. "You're going to let them get away with this?"

"What other choice do we have?" Clay walked over to where she was standing behind the couch and reached for her hands. "Think about it, Carla. You know how your grandfather operates and my grandmother's no dummy, either. Considering how cleverly they've managed things up until now, do you think there's any easy way out of here? I don't know about you, but I'd rather enjoy a pleasant four-day vacation in a picturesque country retreat, than take a grueling hike down the side of a mountain, especially when we don't know what we'd find at the bottom."

"I don't believe it," Carla murmured, stunned that he'd gotten over his anger so quickly and had seemingly resigned himself to his fate. "You're actually willing to look at this as a vacation?"

Clay squeezed her hands and smiled down into her eyes. "To tell you the truth, I can't think of anything I'd rather do than spend some uninterrupted time with you. I'm sure the old folks kept us on the run so we wouldn't stop and question things too closely, but sooner or later, you and I are going to have to talk about what happened last night. I don't know about you, but I think there's something very special going on between us and I think it's worth exploring. Frankly, it doesn't much matter to me who's responsible for this situation. We've been set up but the feelings between us are real. I want to get to know you, Carla, and I want you to know me."

Lowering his head, he dropped a gentle kiss on her lips. "Does that sound so bad?"

Put that way, it sounded wonderful to her, but it still galled her to think that the more she enjoyed herself, the more it would please the two people who had arranged for her and Clay to be together. "How could they do this to us?"

"I've been asking myself the same question and the only answer I can come up with is that they love us." Clay laughed at her dubious expression, preventing her from voicing her protest of that theory by placing two fingers over her lips. "I'll admit that I never expected my grandmother to go to such lengths to make me take a closer look at my life, but now that she has, I can understand her worry."

"You can?"

"I haven't taken a vacation in over six years, Carla. Other than those women my grandmother arranged for me to meet by appointment, I haven't even gone out on a date. Work has been the be-all and end-all of my existence ever since my grandfather died."

Having gained her attention, he lifted his fingers away from her mouth. "As you know, my father doesn't have much of a business sense, but he refused to give up his control of the company and my grandmother didn't want to hurt him by voting against him. Finally, he'd made so many bad oversea investments, we were facing a possible bank failure. It had to reach that point before I was able to convince grandmother to turn her voting power over to me. Relations between me and my father have been strained ever since, but I just couldn't stand idly by and watch everything my grandfather worked a lifetime to build be destroyed by his son's bad business judgment. We've since recovered from our financial problems, but I'm still working as hard and long as I did right after the takeover.''

Looking down into her eyes, he inquired, ''What about you?''

Carla gave a little shrug. ''It takes a lot of hard work to build up a successful business.''

Clay nodded. ''Yes it does, but according to the financial report I had done on your firm, you've been operating in the black for the last three years. How many vacations have you had since you started turning a sizable profit?''

Carla made sure he saw the resentment she still felt over the matter of his investigation before she admitted, ''I've been meaning to take one. I just never seemed to get around to it.''

''And how long has it been since you've been involved with a man?''

Carla flushed at the question. ''Considering that last night was the first time for me, you should know the answer to that!''

Clay's eyes opened wide. ''I realize that you've never gone to bed with anyone, but surely you've done a lot of dating?''

''I wouldn't say a lot,'' Carla replied evasively, embarrassed to admit that her previous relationships with men were pretty much limited to going out to dinner with a client or calling upon a colleague to escort her to a professional function.

She didn't realize how much she was revealing as she tacked on defensively, "Like you, I haven't devoted much time to romance. Ever since I left college and moved to New York, I've concentrated all my energies on making my firm a success."

Making a face at him, she continued, "As you no doubt already know, my parents didn't approve of my decision to leave Boston. Like all the other women in my family, I was expected to get married, have two lovely children and content myself doing charitable works. They were very upset when I broke my engagement to the man they'd picked out for me. They immediately cut off my allowance, assuming I'd give up on the idea of starting my own business and return to the family fold. I suppose that's part of the reason I've worked so hard to achieve my financial independence. I needed to prove that I haven't suffered by my decision."

Clay's expression revealed nothing but admiration for her as she concluded her speech, though he wasn't the least bit pleased to find out that she'd once been engaged. That investigator he'd hired hadn't included that important piece of information in his report and therefore, wouldn't be contacted again. Before he could stop himself, Clay found himself asking, "What was the name of this guy you were engaged to?"

Nose in the air, Carla proclaimed haughtily, "My good man, surely you've heard of Joseph Benton of the Boston Bentons. Why his family is at the very tip-top of the social register."

"But he wasn't tip-top in your book?"

"Tip-top of boring and he kissed like a dead fish," Carla said, unaware that she'd just extinguished the jealous fires that had started burning inside Clay at the mention of the Benton name. Carla was right to assume that he'd heard of the family. The Bentons owned the oldest and largest import-export business on the East Coast and could trace their roots back to the Boston Tea Party. Money, power, prestige—as the eldest son of the family, Joseph Benton had it all.

And Carla found him boring! Clay was elated by the thought until he remembered that she'd had the very same opinion about him not too long ago. Dropping his arms around her waist, he drew her closer to his body. "How would you rate my kisses?"

Mesmerized by the intensity of his gaze and the husky quality in his voice, Carla spoke honestly. "Other than Joseph and a couple of equally chaste young men, I have no basis for comparison."

Clay was shocked. "Are you telling me that I'm the first man who's ever gotten past first base with you!"

"Well, that's a crude way of putting it."

"Is it true?"

"Yes," Carla admitted, completely astonished by Clay's reaction to the information.

"My God," he swore, setting her away from him as if she'd suddenly grown a pair of horns. "And I...Lord!" Clay raked one hand through his hair, turning away from her as he began to pace.

Having watched him exhibit this type of behavior before, Carla knew he wasn't angry with her, but was trying to work out some inner struggle. Something about her disclosure really bothered him. From past experience she knew that it wouldn't do her any good to question him until he'd run out of words.

Taking a seat on the couch, she listened to him berate himself in some very colorful language. One day, she was going to have to ask him who had taught him to swear like a longshoreman. It didn't fit his image of a conservative banker at all. The thought of him pacing inside the boardroom at the Chancelor Bank, spouting phrases that would turn the air blue, made her laugh.

At the sound of her amusement, Clay sat down next to her on the couch. "This isn't funny, Carla. It was hard enough for me to deal with the fact that I was your first lover, but to find out I'm your first *everything* is one hell of a responsibility to deal with. When I think of what happened last night, I could just kick myself."

"Why would you want to do that?" Carla asked, thoroughly confused.

"I tried my best to make some concessions for your innocence, but I never thought you were completely inexperienced. I went way beyond petting in the first thirty seconds!" His face hardened and he couldn't meet her eyes. "You've never felt a man's touch on your breasts and there I was, not only touching but kissing them, them and every other part of you as if you were familiar with all facets of lovemaking. You must have been scared to death."

Carla knew she didn't have much experience when it came to men, but she knew when she was dealing with one of the best examples of the species. She'd heard other women talk about their lovers, listened to comments about how selfish men were when they made love, but Clay wasn't like that at all. He couldn't have been a more considerate lover and her sexual initiation had been the most beautiful experience of her life.

Nothing could have endeared Clay to her more than to hear that he was just as concerned with the state of her mind as he'd been with the state of her body. "Did I act scared?"

"I didn't give you time to be scared. I overwhelmed you with pleasure and then you were too far gone to tell me to slow down." He shook his head guiltily. "And this morning, instead of talking about what had to be the most traumatic experience of your life, I hustled you out of bed to go chasing after the folks. After everything I've put you through in the last two days, I'm amazed you're still talking to me."

"You're an awfully sweet man, Clay Chancelor," Carla said sincerely. His eyes shot to her face and she smiled. "You can overwhelm me with pleasure anytime you like and I won't hold it against you. That's a promise."

The look on his face was so comical, Carla laughed. "I'm a grown woman, Clay, not a child. Believe me, if I didn't like what you were doing to me, you would have heard about it."

Clay appreciated her kind attempt to alleviate some of his guilt, but he knew she was only saying it to make him feel better. Before he'd found out that she was a virgin, he'd seen and felt her fear, and she'd been too frightened to open her mouth. If he hadn't backed off when he had, he would have been guilty of a whole lot more than gross insensitivity. "You're being incredibly understanding, Carla Valentine, but I know better than that. I took advantage of your innocence and you were too helpless to fight me."

"Is that so?"

Clay's eyes went wide at her challenging tone, and wider yet when he felt her hand moving on his thigh. "What are you doing?"

Carla leaned closer until her head was resting on his chest while she caressed him higher and higher on his leg. "Getting even," she murmured sweetly as she felt his helpless response to her touch.

At the sight of Carla's fingers on him, feeling her inching them closer and closer to the ache she created with every caress, Clay stifled a groan. He couldn't seem to do anything but watch in stunned fascination as she finally attained her goal and he felt the heat of her palm on his arousal. He had to tell her to stop, before he lost control, but the words became locked in his throat as he watched her unbuckle his belt and pull down on his zipper. Slowly, so slowly, he was in agony before the task was even halfway completed.

Clay closed his eyes as she eased her hand inside his clothes and his head fell back on the couch as the warmth of her hand embraced him. He let out a ragged, tortured breath, but the sound only served to inspire her to a greater daring. Lovingly, she measured his potency.

"I hope you won't be too angry with me for taking advantage of you like this," she murmured softly. "But then, fair is fair."

"You're incredible," he got out jerkily, unable to endure another second of this sweet, burning torture. Somehow he managed to pull her hands away from his body, but paid for it with each shuddering breath he drew into his lungs. "Forget what I . . . said about protecting your . . . maidenly virtues. I can see now that I'm going to have one hell of a time protecting my own."

"You'd better believe it, buster," Carla verified smugly, just before she was hauled onto his lap and scooped up in his arms.

"This is war, Ms. Valentine," Clay warned, swinging her legs around in one direction, then the other, as he searched for the best place for them to make love.

"How can you ever hope to win if you can't even locate the battlefield?" Carla teased, flinging out her arm to point to a closed door she'd spotted near the daybed. "That way."

"Hmmph," Clay grunted, as he carried her in the direction indicated, adjusted her in his arms so he could open the door only to discover that they'd entered a bathroom. "Looks like you're not that great a field marshall yourself."

"Set me down before you drop me," Carla advised, as Clay struggled to get them both back out the narrow door. "How about if we agree to join forces just until we locate the stairs? There's got to be some around here someplace."

"I'll find them," Clay declared staunchly, lifting her higher in his arms, then swiveling her body around until he could hoist her over one shoulder. "A con-

quering hero like myself would never release a defenseless female until he'd had his way with her.''

"I'll show you defenseless," Carla vowed, but he
anticipated her response and clamped a steely arm
over her legs before she could kick him. Since he
couldn't use the same means to restrain her arms,
Carla gave him a healthy slap on the rump and was
gratified by his yelp.

"Boy, this conquering business is a lot harder than
it sounds," Clay muttered in an aggrieved tone, getting a little short of breath, as he marched around the
perimeter of the room in a fruitless search for the hidden stairs to the second floor.

By the time he'd opened and closed the door to two
clothes closets and a pantry, Carla was laughing so
hard she had trouble talking. "You're almost out of
breath, oh mighty conqueror," she managed between
giggles. "If you'd rather put off pillaging for another
day, I'll certainly understand."

"All my helpless captives say that in hopes of stav-
ing off the inevitable," Clay panted, coming to a stop
in the center of the room. Since he'd checked all the
doors, the only place left to look was the ceiling and
that's where he spotted what looked like a long, rect-
angular trapdoor with an ornamental pull chain
hanging from one side.

"Aha!" he cried out in triumph as he carried his
laughing burden another few feet. A few moments
later, he was puffing up the wooden stairs that had
descended from the ceiling with a yank of the chain.
"After all my labors, this had better be the stairway to
heaven."

And they both agreed it was as they reached the top and Clay lowered Carla to her feet. They'd found a bedroom all right, but it was unlike any bedroom either of them had ever seen. Except for the few feet of plush white carpeting that bordered the octagonal space, the room was all bed.

Each of the ten panels forming the walls was a window, a beautifully designed stained glass window that filtered light into a galaxy of colors that shimmered across the white satin spread and matching pillows. Suspended at an angle over the satin platform were three more panels of glass, forming a trio of skylights.

Clay and Carla looked up at the same time, awed by a magnificent view of the mountains. "I wonder who owns this place?" Clay queried out loud. "And I wonder how much they'd take for it."

"You'd like to buy it?"

"Wouldn't you?"

Yes, she would, Carla realized. "And I saw it first so I get to make the first offer."

"You make an offer and I'll top it," Clay promised.

"Then I'll top that."

"We'll see." Clay shrugged her pledge aside, deciding it was time that they entered into far more pleasurable negotiations. "Remember how I told you that I'd like to keep you in bed for days and days and days."

Carla swallowed nervously, remembering well.

Clay lifted his hand to her face, stroking the delicate bone structure of her jaw with his thumb. "What would you say to four?"

The adoring look in his eyes made Carla feel as if she were melting. And she felt that she had a few seconds later when Clay took her hand and drew her across the remaining few feet to the bed. Her legs simply refused to hold her.

I love him! The thought jolted through her even as she tried to form a response to his question that would not make her sound like a blithering idiot. "Four . . . would be nice."

"For a start," he murmured huskily, as he followed her down on the bed.

Within seconds, their clothing was gone and their merging bodies were adorned by the shimmering spectrum of light that filtered through the stained glass windows. Each straining motion was magnified by dancing color until all their senses were swirling in a blur of amber, magenta and gold.

Carla reveled in a sense of feminine power as she pressed her breasts against Clay's chest and he groaned in pleasure. Her body fit with his perfectly and he reacted to even the slightest movement she made. She shifted her hips and Clay shuddered with the effort of restraint.

"Not yet, Carla. I want this to last," he murmured huskily, taking her breath away as he swiftly rolled off to one side.

In a matter of seconds, Carla was the one who was moaning in pleasure as Clay captured the tip of one breast in his mouth. His tongue swirled around and around until she was gasping, then he administered the same torturous treatment to her other breast. Even when she grasped his shoulders, telling him that she couldn't wait much longer, he showed no inclination to hurry.

Clay took his time, savoring her taste, the texture of her skin, driving her farther as he pressed kisses down the silken length of her body. When his caressing fingers and mouth finally found her moist core, Carla cried out as the spirals within her tightened unbearably.

"Now," she gasped. "I need you now."

Clay couldn't help but respond. She was in perfect rhythm with him, matched him on every level, accepted him as her own.

The mutual intensity of their demands went beyond touch and sound and light as they reached for something far beyond the reach of their senses. Abandoning herself to this fervent quest of discovery, Carla arched her back, pleading for Clay to accompany her, then demanding it. Clay resisted her wild, uninhibited urgings as long as he was able, prolonging the exquisitely sweet agony until she called out his name.

I love you, he repeated over and over in his mind, knowing it was too soon to utter the words, but conveying them to her with his eyes, and his mouth and his body. He thrust into the wild heat of her, taking her up and up into the swirling colors and brilliant light until they were both consumed in a galactic explosion.

It took a long time for the starbursts within them to subside, for the lights to die down and the colors to fade. When they did, Carla opened her eyes, aware that Clay was holding her with an almost bruising strength and that he was still locked deeply within her. He stirred slightly and it was as if she were connected to a powerful electrical current that could easily bring all that brilliance back again.

To her amazement, as Clay shifted his legs, she felt a shocking renewal of tension and an equally shocking need to inspire the same feeling in him. Before either of them had fully recovered, she was urging him to continue. She lifted her hips, twisting slowly, provocatively, shivering with anticipation and remembered pleasure.

"Carla?" Clay groaned, feeling the rippling tremors within her, feeling the heat and the womanly softness tightening around him, drawing him in deeper and deeper. "You want me again?"

"For days and days," she whispered, her voice trembling as she kept him to his promise.

Eleven

By the end of the first day at the cabin, Carla's anger at Freddie had diminished considerably. By the end of the second, she'd almost forgotten her reasons for being upset. By the third, she was enjoying herself too much to be angry with anyone and by the fourth, she wished there was some way to stop the passage of time.

Away from the responsibilities of her work, the demands of her clients and her tight daily schedule, Carla felt more carefree and happy than she had in ages. She was also in love for the first time in her life—hopelessly, helplessly in love. She knew she was living in a romantic dreamworld, that she would have to face up to reality again very soon, but she wanted to hold on to the fantasy as long as she possibly could, almost as much as she wanted to hold on to the man who was sharing it with her.

Clay Chancelor had not only turned out to be the perfect lover, but also the perfect playmate and companion. Freed of his responsibilities at Chancelor Enterprises, he'd switched his considerable energies toward pleasing her and he was as successful at that task as he was at running the family business. Even if their affair came to nothing, and chances were high that it would, Carla would always cherish the memory of these four marvelously idyllic days.

They'd made love several times during the first afternoon and evening, but eventually had left the upstairs bedroom in search of food. They'd found enough provisions in the refrigerator and pantry to feed an army, but instead of making something up from scratch, they'd contented themselves with one of the several premade casseroles and a bottle of good domestic wine.

Shortly thereafter, they'd discovered that food and drink weren't the only things that had been provided for them by their benefactors. After forty-eight hours in the same clothes, they'd almost decided to go native and prance around in the bath towels they'd donned after their shower, when Clay had found several pieces of luggage stored in the front hall closet. To their amazement, the suitcases had not only contained his-and-her toiletries, but several sets of clothing in their correct sizes. All casual clothes, they realized as they'd divided the jeans and shorts, shirts, sweaters, shoes and socks into his-and-her piles.

Curious to see what else their grandparents might have left behind for them, they'd searched all the cupboards, closets and shelves in the house. It was like being on a scavenger hunt, only they didn't know what kind of items they were looking for until they found them. By the end of their search, they'd amassed several board games, a deck of playing cards, a tape player and a collection of classical tapes, a model airplane kit and a number of best-selling paperbacks they'd each been meaning to read but hadn't found the time. Their grandparents had tried to make certain that they would not get bored and they hadn't, but that wasn't due to the recreational aids the elderly couple had provided.

The very first night, Carla and Clay had decided to view their four-day sentence in the cabin as a few stolen days—a brief romantic interlude to be savored and enjoyed to the utmost of their abilities. They'd entered into a pact which declared that for these four days, they would be entirely themselves, totally free to do whatever they wanted, whenever they wanted. They'd quickly found out that they had much more in common than the glorious passion that made them such compatible lovers. They were equally well matched as friends.

After the first day, they'd discovered that they both enjoyed cooking and liked the same kind of foods. Though neither of them liked to clean up after a meal, they were equally adept at coming up with ingenious ways to escape doing their fair share. Later they'd found that they both favored long, leisurely walks over jogging and preferred watching stars to watching television.

In the evenings as they sat before the fire, they'd learned that they had similar views on many subjects,

including politics and religion. They were both work-
aholics, yet they yearned for a more fulfilling personal life, admitting that there were many times when
they found themselves feeling lonely. The more they
talked, the more they realized how much alike they
were, something neither one of them would have accepted considering the occasion of their first meeting.

If dreams could go on forever, Carla knew she
would never have to be lonely again, but all it took was
a glance at the clock to tell her that her time with Clay
was fast running out. It was late in the morning of the
fourth day, and reality would soon come crashing
through the door of their idyllic retreat in the form of
two senior citizens. ''They'll be here soon,'' Carla
said, praying that her feelings didn't show on her face
as she gazed across the table at Clay.

''I know,'' he replied, and poured himself another
cup of coffee.

Carla bit her lip at the curtness of his tone. Ever
since they'd gotten out of bed this morning, there had
been several periods of uncomfortable silence between them. She'd tried several times to engage him in
conversation, but Clay hadn't been very cooperative.
Considering his response to her latest attempt, she
thought better of trying again. Apparently, he didn't
think they had anything left to talk about.

A few moments later, she found out she was wrong,
and she almost jumped out of her chair when he
growled, ''Look! After viewing things from all possible angles, I think we should be good sports about this
and go along with the program.''

Carla didn't have a clue as to what he was trying to say. "I beg your pardon?"

Clay poured the last of the coffee into her empty cup, then banged the pot down in the middle of the table. "I say we make it legal."

"Make what legal?" Carla asked, still not following.

"Let's get married."

Carla choked on a sip of coffee and it took several moments before she'd recovered enough to speak coherently. Clay was obviously joking, but she couldn't go along with the joke. "Sorry, but I'm not quite that good a sport," she declared tightly, latching on to the first argument that came to mind. "We barely know each other."

Clay took offense at her gross misjudgment of their relationship. "We haven't known each other very long," he conceded. "But we've learned more about each other in the last few days than most people find out in years. I've learned enough to know that I really like you, Carla. We've had a great time together and I think we'd make a good couple. I'm pretty sure you feel the same way. So what's the problem?"

What's the problem? Liking isn't love that's the problem she wanted to scream at him, but instead, put forth reasonably, "I like a lot of people, Clay, but that doesn't mean I'd ever consider marriage to them."

Clay felt like he'd just been kicked in the stomach. He'd finally worked up his courage to propose to the woman and she wasn't even willing to think about it? His eyes glowing with temper, he pushed back his chair and stood up. "You refuse to even consider it!

Well, that's great, Carla, just great. We've spent four solid days in bed together, and the thought of marriage never once entered your mind?''

Carla opened her eyes in surprise. ''Are you saying it entered yours?''

Clay heard the incredulity in her question and realized that they'd been on different wave lengths all along. Just as he had from the very beginning with her, he'd once again leaped to some very wrong conclusions. After a long, tense pause, he sat back down in his chair, shaking his head at his own stupidity.

He laughed self-deprecatingly. ''We were good together, very good and not just in bed. So I figured, why not? I'm thirty-three years old, and the thought of getting married and raising a family has been on my mind quite a bit lately. I guess that's why I got so caught up in the idea of playing house with you.''

''If we got married, we wouldn't be playing,'' Carla pointed out.

Clay shrugged as if discarding a momentary flight of fancy. Then he smiled. ''It was fun while it lasted though, wasn't it?''

Carla heard his use of the past tense and a painful lump formed in her throat. For a few seconds, she'd fostered the hope that he was prepared to stand by his proposal, that he'd actually fallen in love with her and couldn't bear the thought of losing her. Considering how quickly he'd retracted the words, that hope swiftly died.

''Yes it was,'' she agreed with a wistful smile, unaware that both her smile and her tone of voice conveyed a fatalistic sense of finality.

Clay stared down into his empty coffee cup, struggling to overcome a wrenching anger. In Carla's mind their affair was over, just like that, as if the last five days had meant nothing to her. After all they'd been through together, all that they'd shared, she was willing to kiss him goodbye and continue on her merry way.

He knew he was going to hate finding out, but he had to ask. "So what were you thinking while I was busy fantasizing about a happy hearth and home?"

Carla realized that Clay had far more experience than she in ending these kinds of affairs, that the sophisticated women he was used to dealing with could probably shrug off their emotions as easily as they discarded last year's fashions, but she wasn't capable of rehashing what had transpired between them as if it were already ancient history. "I was thinking that I'd chosen the best possible man to take my virginity and teach me all there is to know about loving," she answered honestly. "You showed me how beautiful sex can be when two people care more about the other person's pleasure than they do about their own."

Averting her face toward the window, she blinked back her tears. "No matter who I eventually marry, I'll always be grateful to you for that."

"You can keep your gratitude," Clay ground out harshly. "I don't need or want it."

Carla felt the blood drain from her face, but she forced herself to continue even if he didn't want to hear what she had to say. "I know that, but I can't help how I feel. You were so patient and kind with me,

Clay. You made my first time so wonderful. I'll never forget it, or you, as long as I live. I—''

Clay cut her off. ''That's enough!'' he shouted, as he stood up from the table. ''Do you think it helps me to know how much you appreciate my sexual know-how? I'm in love with you, lady, and no matter how you choose to look at it, you were using me.''

''Clay, no, I never—''

''I don't want to hear it,'' Clay interrupted her. ''I feel enough of a fool as it is.''

He gave a bitter laugh. ''God! There I was loving you with every bone in my body and you were seeing me as a kindly professor giving you some useful lessons in sexual technique. And now that you've graduated from my bed, some other lucky man gets to reap the benefits of all I taught you. Well that's dandy, Carla. Just fine and dandy!''

Before Carla could utter a single word in her own defense, he was off. Mouth agape, she just sat there as he stalked away from the table and slammed out the front door, still swearing.

Carla stayed where she was for several minutes, struggling to digest the incredible knowledge that Clay was in love with her. Once she did, she couldn't do a thing about it. The front door opened again, and Clay stepped back inside, but he wasn't alone.

Carla covered her mouth with her hand as she surveyed the appearance of the new arrivals. Lillian Chancelor was dressed in a lovely pink silk dress, pink shoes, white gloves and a wide-brimmed, white straw hat. Freddie wore a dark navy pin-striped suit, white shirt and a dashing silk cravat. They looked like two people who had dressed to attend a wedding and had just found out that they'd walked in on a funeral.

"Our jailers have arrived to set us free," Clay announced sarcastically. "But before we end this ridiculous farce, I for one, would like to hear how it ever came about in the first place. Come on in, both of you, and sit down so we can all have a nice little chat."

"Oh, dear. Things haven't worked out at all well, have they?" Lillian looked stricken as her grandson grasped her elbow and escorted her to the couch.

As soon as she was seated, Clay turned back to Freddie who hadn't moved away from the front door. "Don't worry, I'm past the violent stage."

Freddie cast an anxious glance at Carla who didn't blame him for doubting Clay's word. Every move Clay made, every nuance of expression spoke of a powerful, barely suppressed anger. Thinking her grandfather deserved to suffer a little for all he'd put her through, Carla didn't tell him that she was to blame for Clay's surly attitude. Nor could she do anything to alleviate Clay's foul mood. She couldn't declare her love for him until they were alone.

Getting up from the table, Carla requested in a saccharine tone, "Yes, Grandpa, do come in. Clay and I have so many questions we'd like to ask you."

"Oh dear," Lillian repeated again as her coconspirator acceded to his granddaughter's urgings and reluctantly crossed the room to the couch.

Carla took her place in the leather recliner and to her surprise, Clay sat down on the arm of her chair. Evidently, when it came to this particular confrontation, he was still on her side. Arms folded over his chest, Clay glared over at the couple seated on the couch. "Well?"

For the first time since she'd known him, Carla saw her grandfather at a total loss for words. He cleared his throat, fingered his cravat, crossed and uncrossed his legs, but obviously couldn't think of anything to say that wouldn't land him in even deeper trouble.

"Isn't this just like you, Freddie? The 'Kid' always had to step in and fish you out of the soup and now you expect me to do the same," Lillian complained tartly, displaying more spirit than she had since her arrival.

"The Kid?" Clay inquired.

"Your grandfather, dear," Lillian explained. "He was known in the business as 'Kid Chancelor.'"

Carla gasped at this revelation, well aware of what "business" Lillian was referring to. "You've got to be joking!"

Lillian's smile was like the Cheshire cat's. "It's quite true, dear. Of course, you'll understand if I ask you to treat this as privileged information. The financial world is so judgmental about these sort of things. They like their bankers very conservative and proper."

"Of course," Carla repeated stupidly, glancing at Clay who looked more confused than stunned.

"You're talking about my grandfather?" Clay asked. "My grandfather went under the name of Kid Chancelor? How come I've never heard about this before?"

"It was long before your time, Clay," Lillian said. "And poor Northrop has such a hard time dealing with that aspect of our family history, we tried hard not to mention it. He would much prefer to have people believe that there's not one corpuscle of red blood in our veins and that our fortune was inherited."

Freddie chuckled, so pleased by Clay's and Carla's reaction to the first part of this disclosure that he finally found his tongue to impart the rest. "We were all working Chicago back in the thirties. Times were tough on the streets in those days, but I was running a shell game on Michigan Avenue and doing okay. The Kid didn't go in for that kind of thing. He didn't have to. He was handsome as they come and women were willing to pay just to be seen on his arm."

Freddie patted Lillian's hand, grinning at some memory. "But then the Kid met Lilly and he decided to have his cake and eat it, too. He was afraid one of us might jinx his setup with a lovely heiress so we didn't find out her name 'til after the wedding."

"I was staying at the Wilson House at the time and Barclay was only one of several well-to-do young gentlemen who had come calling," Lillian remembered fondly. "I have no idea how the rumor first got started, but somehow word got out that I had just come into a sizable fortune. I did my best to deny it, but the invitations just kept coming. Suddenly, I found myself the toast of the town."

"She turned down more proposals than most women got in their entire lives. Even refused a Rockefeller," Freddie continued enthusiastically. "Then, not more than a week after she met him, she walked down the aisle with Barclay Chancelor. When the news filtered through the ranks that 'Love-'em-and-leave-'em Lilly' had gone and married Kid Chancelor, I can tell you, it caused quite an uproar. The rest of us practically laughed ourselves silly. Both looking out for the main chance and ending up poor as church mice."

"Poor but happy," Lillian amended.

"Love-'em-and-leave-'em Lilly," Clay mumbled dumbly.

"A very tasteless name," Lillian admitted. "Especially since I was a perfect lady at all times and was never unkind to a rejected suitor. I was true to Barclay from the first moment I met him. Of course, being short on funds did cause some problems for us in the beginning of our marriage. But through our various contacts with those in possession of greater resources, we were able to gather several inside tips on the upward progression of the stock market. Barclay was a charmer and we were always welcome in the best circles. Within five years, we'd accrued enough capital to start the Chancelor Bank."

"Let me get this straight," Clay demanded. "Are you trying to tell me that both you and my grandfather are . . . were—"

"A vamp and a scamp," Lillian supplied cheekily. "And you're so much like him, Clay. I couldn't just sit back and watch while you turned yourself into a stodgy traditionalist like your father. Barclay would have been so proud of what you've been able to accomplish at the bank, but he never would've wanted you to center your whole life on business."

She gazed pointedly at Carla. "Especially when the world has so much more to offer you."

"I don't believe this," Clay muttered.

Lillian sighed, "Somebody had to lay a fire under you. Barclay would never forgive me if I allowed you to continue as you were going. You were really becoming quite boring and stuffy. Your father didn't have it in him to be anything more than he is, but you Clay, you have the potential to live and love as passionately as your grandfather. Before Barclay died, you were always taking chances, but since then you've become appallingly conservative. You definitely needed more adventure in your life."

"Good God." Clay shook his head incredulously.

"I felt much the same way about you, Carla," Freddie announced, as if conservatism was a sin of the greatest magnitude. "When I met up with Lillian again and we compared notes on our grandchildren, we began to think that the two of you could bring out the best in each other. We knew you'd both come running if you believed that we'd gotten engaged, and we suspected that once the two of you met, the sparks would really fly."

"And we were so right," Lillian put in smugly. "But then, Clay started ostrichizing again, so we had to do something to pull his head out of the sand. I can tell you, Barclay never would've let three weeks go by before seeing me again. He would have been very disappointed in you, Clay."

"So you pretended to elope?" Carla questioned, diverting everyone's attention away from Clay who was starting to mutter under his breath.

Lillian nodded. "We called up a few old friends and asked for their help. Of course, the first people we thought of were Lucy and Will in Connecticut and they were happy to help. Lucy's brother Sam offered to lend a hand and so did Harvey since he was one of Barclays' oldest and dearest friends. And they were all so delighted to be working together again.''

"In our younger days, we operated a flying circus together," Freddie declared.

Carla's brows rose another notch higher. "Who did? Not you, Freddie? You don't even have a pilot's license."

Freddie chuckled, "Harv had the license. The Kid had the plane and Lucy looked swell in tights. I was the hawker. I stayed on the ground and kept the crowds in awe of the death-defying feats going on up in the air. Lucy danced on one wing and Barclay stood on his head on the other. It was a great act."

"I wish I could have seen that," Lillian took the words right out of Carla's mouth. "But the troupe had gone on to other occupations by the time I met them."

Even Clay couldn't hide his interest. "Grandpa was an aerialist?"

"In those days, it paid to be diversified," Freddie informed him. "Barclay was probably a better pilot than Harv, but Harv couldn't stand on his head for beans. Now Will got pretty good at hanging upside down from the axle rod, but Lucy put up such a fuss every time he went up in the air that we let him work the crowd instead."

"Some things never change," Clay remarked dryly and Carla giggled.

At the sound of her laugh, Clay's jaw went tense. "Enough about your past exploits. How would you like to hear how your present scheme worked out?"

"You needn't bother, Clay," Lillian sniffed. "It's humiliatingly apparent that you bungled it."

"*I* bungled it!" Clay shot to his feet. "Grandmother, I swear, if I didn't love you so much I'd...I'd..."

"I know exactly how you feel," Carla offered sympathetically, though Clay's expression revealed that he didn't appreciate the offer. "Freddie often has the same effect on me."

Freddie clapped one hand over his breast and misquoted, "Oh, how sharper than a serpent's tooth it is to have a thankless grandchild."

"I'd rather have a thankless one than one who lets foolish pride stand in the way of his happiness," Lillian declared.

Suddenly, her blue eyes met Carla's and a silent communication took place between them. Carla didn't know how the older woman could tell, but it was obvious that Lillian was well aware that her efforts at matchmaking had been a resounding success. A few seconds later, the two women exchanged smiles of perfect understanding, and then Lillian observed, "At least Carla has managed to maintain her delightful sense of humor throughout this ordeal."

"And ordeal is exactly the right word for it," Clay growled.

Carla wrinkled her nose at him. "Thank you for your vote of confidence, Lillian."

Clay made a nasty comment that everyone ignored.

"I'm sure you're ready for some refreshments after your long drive from Connecticut," Carla said. "Can I offer you both some tea and a sandwich?"

Lillian gave her grandson a severe glare, then turned back to Carla. "Under such trying circumstances, it's very gracious of you to offer, my dear. And I apologize for the bad manners of my grandson. I hope he hasn't made these last four days too difficult for you."

"Not at all," Carla assured her as she rose from her chair, sidestepped an openmouthed Clay and made her way toward the kitchen.

Clay was breathing down the back of her neck every step of the way, and Carla wasn't the least bit surprised when she heard his harsh whisper in her ear. "What the hell do you think you're doing?"

She whispered back, "You heard your grandmother, I'm being gracious and polite under very trying circumstances. I'm also attempting to hurry this along a little."

"Hurry what along?" Clay inquired, a bit more loudly.

"Well I don't know about you, but I find it a trifle disconcerting to have our grandparents here in the midst of our love nest. If we feed them, maybe they'll leave so I can propose to you in private."

"Huh?" Clay knew that he'd been flirting with insanity all morning, but now he realized he'd slipped over the edge. He thought he'd just heard Carla telling him she was going to propose, so he obviously wasn't hearing right. And he wasn't seeing right either or she wouldn't be looking at him as if she was planning to ravage his body any second. And he most definitely couldn't be feeling her lips kissing his cheek as she passed by him on the way to the stove.

"On second thought, Carla, we really can't stay," Lillian announced from the living-room area as she and Freddie rose from the couch. "It's a long drive back to New York and we'd like to get home before dark."

Carla immediately removed the teakettle from the stove and shut off the burner. "I understand. We can have tea together some other time."

As Carla left the kitchen area she took hold of Clay's arm and urged him to accompany her to the front door. "Have a safe trip you two," she said, releasing Clay's arm so she could step forward and give her grandfather a hug. "And Freddie, please stay out of trouble, at least until we get home."

Lillian walked up to Clay since he seemed incapable of either movement or speech. "I love you, too, darling," she murmured, blue eyes shining with moisture as she went up on tip-toe to bestow a kiss on his cheek. "You've made me so happy. And to think it happened right here in the cabin where Barclay and I spent our honeymoon."

Moving to Carla, she said, "Forgive us, dear. But sometimes the end more than justifies the means."

"There's nothing to forgive," Carla assured as she leaned over to kiss Freddie.

"You're sure?" Freddie whispered, casting a dubious eye in Clay's direction.

"Very sure."

As the older couple said the last of their goodbyes and walked out the door, she called after them. "And don't worry, we'll be in touch very soon. I promise."

"Okay, I'll bite," Clay began as soon as he heard their car start up. "Why are we still here in this cabin while our only source of transportation drives away?"

Carla didn't waste any time telling him. "Because I love you, Clay Chancelor, every bit as much as you love me and now that we're alone again, I intend to prove it."

Clay hesitated for only a second, a half-puzzled, half-certain look on his face as he gazed into her eyes. What he saw there must have convinced him that she was telling the truth for he opened his arms to her. "So what are you waiting for?"

Carla launched herself into his arms, her eyes shining with joy. "I love you, I love you, I love you," she murmured before his mouth came down to intercept the words. When at last they came up for air, Carla stepped back, then went down on one knee before him. "After viewing this thing from all possible angles, I say we be good sports about this and go along with the program. Whaddya say we make it legal?"

"That has to be the all-time most romantic proposal I've ever heard in my life," Clay declared feelingly. "How could any person possibly refuse such a heartrending plea?"

"I know I couldn't, but the man who offered it to me, proposed first and forgot to mention love."

"How remiss of him."

Carla's lips curved into a smile. "Romantic that I am, I really needed those three little words."

"I'll make sure that you hear them often."

"As hard as it's been for me to accept, I think I must take after my grandfather, who as you know, is also incurably romantic. Now who do you suppose you take after?"

Clay laughed as he drew her up before him, then bent over and swung her up into his arms. As he pulled the chain that brought the stairs down from the ceiling, he stated proudly, "I take after a dashing, impetuous guy by the name of Kid Chancelor and if I work fast, I could beat his record for sweeping beautiful young vamps off their feet."

"I bet he'd be proud to know that you were the one to break his record," Carla replied solemnly, as she was carried up the stairs. "And if we have a son, maybe he could try breaking yours."

"Sounds like the start of a great tradition," Clay agreed, a wondering expression on his face as he thought about Carla pregnant with his child.

Carla kissed the side of his neck. "It will be up to us to ensure that the next generation of our family shows the proper respect for this time-honored tradition."

"Yes indeed," Clay acknowledged as he laid her down on the bed. "And since I intend to start work on producing a new generation right away, we have no choice but to get married as soon as possible."

"No problem," Carla murmured as he joined her. "I happen to know of a delightful little chapel in Connecticut."

"Perfect," Clay whispered, and a day later it was, for as everyone knows, all records are made to be broken.

* * * * *

Silhouette Desire
COMING NEXT MONTH

#379 MIDNIGHT RAMBLER—Linda Barlow
Headmistress Dany Holland had suspicions about Max Rambler.
Vampires belonged in storybooks, but when strange nocturnal events
threatened her students, she was determined to find out Max's secret.

#380 EAGLE'S PREY—Lucy Gordon
Photographing eagles had brought Sara to Farraway Island, but it
was Rorke Calvin who kept her there. His plans for revenge were
almost ripe—could she convince him to give them up for love?

#381 GIVE AND TAKE—Anna Schmidt
Set designer Marlo Fletcher was asked to dress the windows of
Carrington's department store. Sparks flew between her and
Josh Carrington—who would think that matters of the heart were
such a give-and-take business?

#382 NO LAUGHING MATTER—Marie Nicole
Writer Marti McGregor lived by her wit and spent a lot of time hiding
behind it. Producer Stephen Townsend was determined to break
through her defenses—for love was no laughing matter.

#383 CARNIVAL MADNESS—Erin Ross
Tired of nothing but parties, Elizabeth fled the latest Venetian
costume ball, only to find herself in the arms of a waiting gondolier.
Roberto was nothing that he seemed... but all that she desired.

#384 LOST AND FOUND—Robin Elliott
Kendra had no intention of getting involved with her neighbor *or* his
pet rabbit. But Joseph wasn't about to let this enchanting woman
misplace the love he'd searched a lifetime to find!

AVAILABLE NOW:

Silhouette Intimate Moments

Starting in October...

SHADOWS ON THE NILE

by

Heather Graham Pozzessere

A romantic short story in six installments from best-selling author Heather Graham Pozzessere.

The first chapter of this intriguing romance will appear in all Silhouette titles published in October. The remaining five chapters will appear, one per month, in Silhouette Intimate Moments' titles for November through March '88.

Don't miss "*Shadows on the Nile*"—a special treat, coming to you in October. Only from Silhouette Books.

Be There!

IMSS-1